Daggers

Other books by Roger J. Green

The Fear of Samuel Walton
The Lengthening Shadow
The Devil Finds Work
They Watched Him Die
The Throttlepenny Murder
Dreamgold
She Was a Witch
Wolfecho
Cuckoos

Daggers

Roger J. Green

OXFORD
UNIVERSITY PRESS

OXFORD
UNIVERSITY PRESS

Great Clarendon Street, Oxford OX2 6DP

Oxford University Press is a department of the University of Oxford.
It furthers the University's objective of excellence in research, scholarship,
and education by publishing worldwide in

Oxford New York
Athens Auckland Bangkok Bogotá Buenos Aires Calcutta
Cape Town Chennai Dar es Salaam Delhi Florence Hong Kong Istanbul
Karachi Kuala Lumpur Madrid Melbourne Mexico City Mumbai
Nairobi Paris São Paulo Singapore Taipei Tokyo Toronto Warsaw

and associated companies in Berlin Ibadan

Oxford is a registered trade mark of Oxford University Press
in the UK and in certain other countries

First published 2000

British Library Cataloguing in Publication Data available

ISBN 0 19 271828 2

Typeset by AFS Image Setters Ltd, Glasgow
Printed in Great Britain

Do not go gentle into that good night,
Old age should burn and rave at close of day;
Rage, rage, against the dying of the light.

Though wise men at their end know dark is right,
Because their words had forked no lightning they
Do not go gentle into that good night . . .

from 'Do not go gentle into that good night'
by Dylan Thomas

So, still alive she rots. A heart of granite
Would melt at this unmeaning sequel. Lord,
How can this be justified, how can it
Be justified?

from 'My Mother's Sister' by C. Day-Lewis

One

Caroline eyeballed the solicitor, staring at him with evil intensity, fixing him with what her grandmother called 'One of our Caroline's dagger looks'. The man, thought Caroline, was like one of the worst kinds of politicians that sometimes slithered across the family television screen. Thin mean lips, thick lenses to his spectacles so you could not see his eyes and their expression. Caroline's eyes flickered in disgust to the plastic imitation books behind him and her glare sharpened with contempt. Everything in the room was plastic. Including him.

She felt so cross that she squeezed her plastic cup too hard. There was a goblin-like pistol crack and a thin stream of the poisonous coffee stained the clean blouse her mother had made her put on for the visit. The daggers vanished from her eyes. Caroline squirmed with confusion and began to blush.

She heard her father suck in his breath with a toothy whistle of anger as he saw the coffee begin to drip. Father and daughter were not on the best of terms these days. Caroline, very red now, transferred her anger from the solicitor to her father. All her father thought about was money money money. He measured all his life with money. In fact, thought Caroline, warming to her attack, he's like an old tatty money bag himself, soiled, sagging and ready to be chucked away. This made her smile. Her father thought it was a smirk and the furrows above his nose deepened to a frown. He couldn't do a thing with Caroline these days. Then he let his gaze drop and he listened to the solicitor with growing amazement. Caroline, however, did not hear a word the solicitor said. She was too busy trying to wither her father with her stares. Not a single word registered.

'I give to my great-niece CAROLINE FAY WALTON of 63a Limewood Avenue, Eastcaster, my thanks and gratitude for ending for me a lifetime of suffering with her comfort and love. I give to her free of inheritance tax and absolutely my property known as Well Cottage, Church Lane, Lambton, including the furnishing and contents thereof . . . '

Caroline was still not listening to a word. Her mother had once agreed with a schoolteacher that Caroline 'suffers from attention deficit syndrome' and Caroline had never forgiven her. Caroline rarely listened to people she was supposed to listen to. Besides, her father was much more interesting. She could not believe the effect her icy stare was having on him, the icy stare that had replaced the cool smile. Her father was sitting up very straight now and staring at the solicitor with disbelief. Caroline congratulated herself that she had got to him, made him unable to stare back. Once more she missed the vital words.

'And I also leave to the said CAROLINE FAY WALTON my fields in the Parish of One Ash in the County of Derbyshire, west of the farm known as Moonfields Farm, the fields known as Daisy Field, Mouse Park, Elbow, and Butterfield . . . '

Her father looked as if he was about to be sick. Caroline was utterly absorbed with him and did not hear that she had been left in the Will two barns, a stable, a sheep pen, and a cow shed. Then she realized that it was not her hate rays that were upsetting her father. It was something else. He suddenly got to his feet and leaned across to the mean little man behind the imitation wood desk.

'You're telling me that the old fool altered her Will at the last minute and left the whole bloody lot to . . . Caroline?'

Caroline was intrigued to see that saying her name aloud appeared to cause her father a mild asthma attack. Then the detonation of her father's plastic coffee beaker redirected her gaze and she watched with no small satisfaction the brown liquid splash on to the thin blue carpet. His next words convinced her that she had missed some vital knowledge.

'So Caroline's got everything? Cottage, fields, money, shares, the lot? The old fool must have been out of her mind. I shall have a long talk with my daughter here. She hardly knew the old woman except to see her near the end. As I said, I'll have a long talk with madam here and then we'll see about contesting the Will and going back to the original one that left the bulk to me.'

At the mention of 'madam' Caroline switched back on her dagger stare and stared defiantly at her father. The lips of the solicitor parted in a polite meaningless smile but nobody could see his expression and guess what his advice to Caroline's father would be.

Two

'Well, I think it's cruel. I'd finish Aunt Clara off. If you kept a dog alive in the condition she's in you'd be crucified by the *Sun* as a monster. She's got cancer. She's got Parkinson's disease that makes her shake all the time. She's got arthritis in her legs and back and now she's had this stroke or something and she has to stay in a wheelchair. I'd put her to sleep. I'd—'

'Oh, for Christ's sake, Caroline. I only asked you to call in with some Kleenex and Lucozade to the nursing home. That's all I asked. Just for once I wanted you to do something to help and we get all this . . . this euthanasia stuff. Have you written an essay on it in RE or something?'

Caroline was to look back at this particular row. It was one row in a grim bouquet of barbed rows that happened in her fourteenth year. She was to recall its brevity, ferocity, and consequences.

Caroline confronted her mother with uncontrolled loathing. They were in the kitchen and her mother was standing by a small peak of dirty washing. A pile of clothes ready for ironing tottered on a nearby surface. A queue of beakers waited patiently by the dishwasher. On the big kitchen table the piles of exercise books waited to be marked, spanning the table like a ruined blue maze. Her mother tossed her head and stared out of the big Victorian windows into the long garden. Out there the grass needed mowing. Caroline looked out too and saw the unwatered terracotta containers with withered wallflowers and gasping tulips. The lushness of late May had defeated her mother but the garden itself was a riot of green and wet lilacs.

'You could go, Caroline. You do nothing to help.'

'No. I'm sorry. I can't at the moment.' Caroline luxuriated in the exquisite pleasure of refusing to do something. Her mother slowly sank on to a kitchen chair and began to cry with sheer exhaustion.

'I said I was sorry.' Caroline hid her guilt and disgust at her mother's tears by trying to sound calm and reasonable. But the feelings remained and would not mix, a bit like oil and water, as she looked at her mother. The shapeless jumper, the leggings, and the half-moon glasses that Caroline thought were the ugliest things since Adam and Eve. All these fuelled the guilt, deepened the disgust. But it was true what she had said about her great-aunt. She was ill and unhappy and did not seem to want to live.

But there was more. Caroline did not like the old woman. Aunt Clara was her father's aunt. He had taken Caroline to see her when she was small. Taken her to the picture postcard cottage in the heart of the Derbyshire Peak District. The dislike Clara and Caroline had felt for each other had been instant. A neat chemical reaction. Aunt Clara had glanced at Caroline, the little girl.

'She's plenty of weight on her, Jack. A real Walton. She'd have done well mucking out on the old farm.'

Little Caroline declared hate for eternity. She was going through a fat stage and had had a secret Rolo binge on the back seat on the drive out. So Aunt Clara was placed securely on the Top Twenty of Hate. And along with Aunt Clara Caroline had included the antique furniture, the old horse brasses, Sheffield silver plate—everything Aunt Clara had was included.

'She's worth a small fortune,' her father had remarked dreamily and contentedly as they returned to the car. Caroline, a small podgy Caroline, reached for the Rolos and chewed savagely, planning death and destruction for Aunt Clara, falls off cliff tops and lightning bolts.

'I'm sorry, mother. I said I was busy and I am.' The sound of her sweet reason boosted her confidence and she added a barb. 'Besides, she's your relation.'

Her mother reached for a small chopping board, swept off some dry garlic cloves and suddenly hurled the board with a surprisingly loud bang on the pine floorboards of the kitchen. It made a very loud bang. A slight quiver of fear darted through Caroline. Her mother had never done such a thing before. But then, she had never been as awkward as she was being now. Her mother was crying freely.

'Caroline, I really can't stand any more. I really can't. I've so much to do. Going down there to the Home every day is the last straw. I just can't cope. All I asked was that you should take two items for me . . . give me some help . . . '

'It's your duty, Caroline.'

Her father had entered stage left from the hall, frowning, stern, playing the Victorian father. Caroline was glad to turn away from her mother who was in fact beginning to make her feel very miserable. She turned to her father who seemed to do nothing but frown at her these days and tell her off. Caroline had once seen her father with the girls from his office in a pub at Christmas, all smiles, playing Mr Nice Guy. He was no longer Mr Nice Guy to Caroline. Pushing her mother's sobbing to one side Caroline directed all her feelings to her father.

'What's it got to do with duty? Greed is the word you should use. All you're interested in is her money.'

Caroline surveyed the map of her father's face like an experienced general would survey his battle map. She decided her missile had reached its target. A red stain of anger on her father's face revealed the extent of the damage. For a few seconds she had immobilized him.

A sudden thought diverted Caroline. Did her great-aunt know her father wanted her money? She knew every evening her mother had dutifully and wearily visited the old aunt. By the time of the visit the old woman was drowsy with painkilling drugs. And every evening Clara had opened her eyes, unfocused and dull with medication. Every evening the aunt had searched her mind and said the same words to her mother. 'I've very sad news for you, Brenda. Jack's dead.'

Said every night for a month this had chilled and upset Caroline's mother. But then she became used to hearing her husband and Caroline's dad was dead and it became a joke to be told at dinner parties, over coffee in the staffroom. Laughed at over red wine. Caroline had thought it funny from the beginning. She still did and smiled.

'Don't you grin at me, young lady,' roared her father. Caroline could see her father would like to have smacked her. In fact she was sure he was going to smack her. He blamed Caroline utterly for the weeping wife and mother. Caroline stepped back, fear and fascination combining inside her.

A very loud knock on the back door ended the performance. Caroline felt a surge of relief. Events had been slipping out of control. Now she was in charge again. Her parents were both confused, angry that a visitor might have heard the private family warfare. Feeling safe and poised again Caroline opened the back door with a flourish.

To Caroline it was only Edward from next door, four years older than her, but always a friend right from the days they had raced worms together in the sandpit. To her parents it was Edward, son of Professor Robson the next-door neighbour, a man they spent their lives trying to impress. Wondering what Edward had heard they stammered and muttered and Caroline's mother turned away hastily to let a tea towel absorb the tears. Caroline took over. She liked Edward very much. In fact her feelings for him were very much deeper but she would only admit this to herself in very private moments. Now she gave him a dazzling smile.

'Hi, Edward. Will you do me a favour? Give me a lift to Aunt Clara's nursing home?'

Edward nodded agreeably. He had just passed his driving test and was at the happy stage of driving everybody where they wanted to go whenever they wanted to go. He had in fact come round to ask Caroline if she wanted to go for a drive. He owed her a favour. He was at Sixth Form College and Caroline, who was a brilliant artist, had designed him a very impressive cover for his Biology fieldwork.

Caroline glowed. She gently pushed her father aside (now completely defused in Edward's presence) and snatched up the Lucozade and Kleenex.

'I'll take these down, mother. Now Edward's taking me it's made all the difference.' She smiled sweetly at both her parents and left, slamming the door with what her father would call 'an impertinent bang'.

Three

It was Caroline's second visit to the nursing home. She had been before with her mother, remaining silent and shocked at what she saw. Clara, now in her nineties, had lived in the cottage with home helps to cook, bath, and dress her. Then came the stroke and a crying, shaking, and paralysed Clara was deposited in the home. Caroline felt her old dislike of the woman mix with a great sadness. All she wanted to do was escape and forget all about Clara. But today it was a way of capturing Edward and she could see he was interested: he wanted to be a doctor. Caroline led the way. As she had said to her mother, Edward made all the difference.

There were ordinary bedrooms but Clara was in a room that was more like a hospital room with special bed and a panel of graphs and dials above the bed. Clara sat in a wheelchair in the room. Here she received treatment until the late morning when she joined the other old people. Caroline's mother had fetched some furniture from the cottage to make the room 'look more like home'. In fact it made it look more of a nightmare. A picture of a carthorse, some brass candlesticks, and a horse brass above a drip made the place appear surreal, a bad dream.

'Hello, Aunt Clara,' said Caroline brightly, sweetly, more for Edward's benefit than the old woman's. 'Mum's sent you these.' She placed the Kleenex and Lucozade before Clara who surveyed them like a carved Indian goddess. She did not speak.

'It's a nice day.' Caroline spoke loudly as she would to a foolish child.

Clara said nothing.

From the next bay, out of the door and left of a big vase of daffodils, came another old woman's voice. 'Oh dear. Oh dear oh dear oh dear. Oh dear oh dear oh dear. Oh dear. Oh.' A mad sad wood pigeon moaning in the forest of wards. Caroline shifted uncomfortably.

'You've got a nice view from your window.' Caroline was losing her confidence. Aunt Clara said not a word. There was a silence save for the quavering wood pigeon cry next door. 'Oh dear oh dear. Oh dear dear oh dear oh dear.' Caroline wanted to run screaming already. Her eyes darted nervously round the room. She saw her aunt's Talking Book machine, saw the tape, saw the label. *Great Expectations* by Charles Dickens. They had been made to read this in class and Caroline was awestruck that anyone, even Aunt Clara, would ever dream of listening to such boring rubbish.

'Shall I pour you a drink of Lucozade, Aunt Clara?'

No reply. Still the wild melancholy, 'Oh dear oh dear,' piped sadly from next door.

'Would you like a tissue, Aunt?' Caroline yanked at the box, pulled, and half the contents burst forth.

'Oh dear oh dear oh dear.' Still her aunt said not a word. Caroline could see that even the confident, suave Edward was beginning to lose his cool.

'I need the toilet,' said the aunt suddenly, straightforwardly. Her voice was treacly and blurred, brain and tongue struggling to connect through damaged circuits. Caroline was tongue-tied too but from sheer incapacity to know what to do. Edward saw more. He saw the red button on a little box at the end of a black wire. He handed it to Clara. She dropped it. Edward picked it up and handed it to her again. It was dropped once more. Edward picked it up and held it. Caroline and Edward watched, as though it were the most important thing in the universe, as Clara concentrated. With tremendous effort she brought a shaking finger towards the button. Caroline found she was holding her breath as the finger slowly aimed for its target. 'Oh dear oh dear,' came the crooning voice. Clara pressed the button. Edward sat back with a sigh, curiously elated. Then all three of them sat there like children in an enchanted wood waiting to see what would happen next. But nothing did for two minutes except the song of the sad wood pigeon.

A woman came and took the brake off the wheelchair. Nothing was said. The wheelchair set off with a squeak on the tiles.

'You've taken your time,' said Aunt Clara, each word carefully announced.

'I can't just drop everything, Clara,' said the woman. 'There's others besides you.'

Caroline found herself criticizing the woman, hating her big bottom as she wheeled her aunt away. She saw her aunt try to turn, unable to, but still able to switch on a dagger look that was so like her own. When they were alone Caroline and Edward found they could not speak to each other. Words had drained out of their brains in the place. Perhaps that was why the aunt would not speak.

Clara returned, wheeled by another woman. Edward thought Clara looked like Queen Victoria in a rage. He also thought that Caroline and her aunt looked the same when they were cross but he kept that observation to himself. This time the woman was pleasant and friendly and smoothed and fussed. She did her best to be caring.

'How nice of you to visit your aunt and bring your boyfriend,' said the woman, smiling as she went away. Caroline and Edward laughed. Caroline was secretly elated. Aunt Clara shut her eyes. Caroline looked at her watch and decided she would stay another fifteen minutes. They sat for a time in silence with only the Oh Dear Pigeon rippling the drowsy silence. Then they began to talk softly, gossip. Talk of boyfriends made them talk about who was going with who in the district. Clara seemed fast asleep. They talked of boyfriends and girlfriends and Caroline tried not to ask whom Edward fancied. She did not want to know what girl was on his mind. Edward was not so tactful.

'I saw you were at Robert's the other night.'

Caroline wished he hadn't. She quickly decided she would tell the truth. 'Yes, I was helping him sort out a new guitar he's bought.' That was true. And it was true that next to Edward she liked Robert very much.

'He says he thinks he's gay,' said Edward in a matter-of-fact voice. He gave it as a fact, a contribution to the gossip. No malice in his tone. But Caroline was thrown into a red sea of confusion. She felt a fool. She felt a red wash of confusion rise from the neck of her T-shirt and spread over her face, a plague of shame. Her face burned. She had, she thought, made a real fool of herself and with Edward of all people.

'Oh . . . Edward . . . I didn't know . . . that.' She managed to say that, try her best to sound unconcerned. She felt the mega-blush engulf her whole body.

Then they were both aware that Clara was awake and very agitated. A drool of saliva was dribbling from the paralysed side of her mouth. She was struggling to talk. The Parkinsonian shaking became horribly noticeable. Caroline and Edward forgot their gossip and watched in consternation. Clara managed to say some words.

'I was responsible for the death of a gay man once. I know I was. People would say I murdered him. I know I did. I killed him . . . ' Her voice trailed away. She gathered her strength. 'His name was Edward. And I killed him.'

There was silence. Even the wood pigeon words of 'oh dear' stopped. Edward and Caroline became as still as statues. They were hypnotized by the laboured breathing of Clara who was struggling to say more but was unable to. After a dose of eternity the woman who had returned with Clara from the toilet poked her head around the entrance.

'Everything OK in here, then?'

'I murdered him and I shall burn in Hell,' said Clara with fearful deliberation, a sentence that took nearly half a minute to say and held everyone in grim concentration. Then the wood pigeon began again its sad call. The care assistant was brisk and cheerful.

'Now don't start again, Clara. We don't want to know that. It's not nice for your visitors, is it? And we know it's not true, don't we? We know we're being a bit silly. You've never hurt anyone in your whole life, darling. You're a bit mixed up with your words, sweetheart.'

'I did. I did. You don't understand.' The words were spoken as though Clara's mouth was clogged with cloth. Her face turned to Edward and Caroline and the expression of pleading shocked and cut into them.

'Just a minute. We'll get something to calm her down. Don't worry.' The auxiliary flashed a professional smile and was gone. Caroline and Edward were left with a shuddering old woman racked by sobs and Parkinson's tremors.

Caroline, who had begun the day by feeling totally in command of herself and her parents, began to cry. She could not cope with this. She wanted to run out and never never return. It was horrible. Her aunt's shaking dislodged the tape container of *Great Expectations*. It fell to the floor. What happened next seemed straight out of the pages of Dickens. A frail, skeleton-thin old woman drifted in and stood at the bottom of Clara's bed, a cobweb fragment from a time and life long before Caroline and Edward. It spoke in a parched dry quivering of air in thin ancient throat.

'What time's lunch?'

'Half past twelve,' said Clara with sudden strength, her apparent murder confession forgotten. Edward and Caroline, sunk in a sea of concern for Clara, surfaced and gulped in breaths of amazement. Perhaps the old woman was confused.

'And tea? What time's tea?' pleaded the ghost, creaking in both voice and body.

'Four,' said Clara in a tone Caroline reserved for her father on bad days.

'Oh my God,' said the ghost. 'Such long, long days . . . ' Voice and ghost trailed away, painfully thin legs in tiny red slippers, dress hanging on thin coat-hanger bone shoulders. Caroline could feel streaks of dried tears on her cheeks. She discovered her mouth was open and shut it lest Edward should see her childlike reaction.

'She was a famous doctor once,' said Clara following the retreat of the spectre with critical eyes. 'Look what this place has done to her. I could have been a doctor once. I could have gone to college. They all said I was clever. But God punished me for murdering Edward.'

Edward and Caroline stared helplessly. Conversation was murdered too. A nurse, straight from a TV commercial for private health care, rustled in with a smile as smart as her uniform. The expensive professional smile was carefully shared out to all in the room. Tablets rattled, glasses flashed, water gleamed, smiles dazzled, tablets were taken and the room swept clean of disturbing thoughts. Clara's paralysed hand was placed under a soft white pillow, her lips and forehead wiped with a cool hospital wipe, she was gently shaken with the pillows at her back into comfort. Then the nurse turned her back on Clara in the manner of a lioness guarding its prey.

'Clara is a very, very old lady,' said the nurse. 'She's had a massive stroke and this has reduced the blood flow to her brain. A stroke in the very old always leads to confusion. She also has Parkinson's disease and is on a high dose of dopamine. This brings on symptoms of schizophrenia. They imagine things, see things or imagine they have done bad things and will be punished. And Clara is also on a low dose of morphine for her cancer and arthritis pain. This causes wild imaginings. She frequently tells us she could have been the cleverest doctor in England or she has just had a cocktail with Marilyn Monroe in New York.'

Caroline glanced nervously at Aunt Clara as the nurse's low urgent lecture ceased. She saw Clara's mouth was in an O mode as she tried to hear what the nurse was saying about her. Caroline felt as battered and buffeted as if she had been in a Florida hurricane.

The nurse suddenly swung back on Clara like a wind vane turning in a gale.

'Feeling better now, Clara dear? I'll take you to the lounge. You can give your guests coffee. There's home-made flapjack this morning.' The nurse released the wheelchair brake like a thunderclap and Caroline jumped. 'You want your handbag, dear? Of course you do. This way.'

Caroline followed obediently. Windbag the nurse may be but she had spoken to Caroline in a grown-up way. The nurse continued to speak over her shoulder as Clara was whisked with professional racetrack skills to the lounge.

'Isn't it warm? The sun's like the Med today. Do you learn about global warming at school? I'm beginning to believe in it myself.'

An hour ago Caroline would have given a very rude reply to an enquiry about school. It always made her feel babyish. But now her confidence was shaken and she could think of nothing to say. The nurse stopped suddenly and Caroline almost went smack into her crisp back and bottom. Peering round she saw another old woman had erupted from a room and was blocking the way.

The little old woman was immaculate in clothes she had bought in the sixties. Wasplike in a yellow and black twinset, hair a dandelion clock of precision perming, she barred the way.

'That's my bed. And that's my wardrobe,' said the woman defiantly and moved back to her door to guard it.

'I don't want it,' said Clara. Caroline suddenly laughed and felt better. She saw herself at ninety-three. She'd be like that, just like Clara. She warmed to her aunt for a few seconds, identified with her as she saw the other old woman off.

'It's a beautiful room, Ethel,' said the nurse and they gathered speed again like an InterCity express that had been momentarily delayed. Arrival in the lounge brought them into a different world again. Here was normality. The Nursing Home had once been the home of a wealthy clockmaker. Large windows opened on to striped lawns and a serene grandfather clock made the passing of time deceptively innocent. Late narcissi drifted beyond the lawns under old willow trees that showed glimpses of the river. Caroline and Edward found themselves seated round a low polished coffee table with a big white coffee pot and both were uncertain how they had been manoeuvred there. The air hummed with conversation. An old lady was giving pocket money to her grandchildren. Two old men were discussing something from a newspaper.

'Will you be mother?' said the nurse and vanished with a Cheshire cat smile before Caroline could think of a scalding reply to such a sexist request. Looking up she saw Aunt Clara follow the nurse's retreat with poisonous eyes and she laughed again. And poured the coffee. She hoped she could still give looks like that when she was ninety-three.

Edward, silent from events, was still cool. He saw the ugly plastic safety cup was for Clara, like a toddler's cup with a safety spout. He filled it and handed it to Clara. Caroline poured for herself and Edward into elegant white cups. The coffee was surprisingly good.

'Sugar,' said Clara. 'One spoonful.' Edward undid the lid, added sugar, replaced the lid. Clara received the plastic cup and drank.

'I want you to go to my cottage,' she said suddenly. 'Your father has a key . . . I don't want him to know you've been . . . Go on your own.' She looked out of the window with the air of a person talking trivia about the weather. 'More coffee.' Edward unscrewed the plastic, poured coffee, screwed the lid back on. 'Sugar,' said Clara. Edward undid the lid. Added sugar. Screwed the thing back. Caroline watched in silence making a mental note to tell her father how disgusted she was with the deplorable manners of the oldest generation. Please and thank you had been lost in the journey to old age.

'Don't tell him . . . don't say a word . . . Go to my back bedroom and feel up the chimney . . . There's a George the Fifth coronation tin up there . . . Bring it here.'

'Please,' said Caroline and then bit her lip. The word had escaped her big mouth like a mischievous parrot escaping its cage.

'Please,' said Clara. She looked at Caroline and Caroline looked back. Identical blue eyes except that one pair was faded with the sunlight of ninety years of living. It was almost half a minute before the aunt looked away and turned to Edward.

'Flapjack . . . please.' Edward held the plate. Edward and Caroline watched the hand flutter and circle over the flapjack. Both thought the hand took less time to land than the time with the button. Eventually the flapjack reached the mouth and was pressed into its destination. Edward thought he could see the faintest of smiles.

Four

Both Caroline and Edward were unable to speak when they returned to Edward's car. The experience with Aunt Clara was quite unlike anything else they had dealt with. Caroline felt like she had once done when she had swum too far off the Norfolk coast and felt nothing but water beneath her feet. She watched Edward fiddle with his new keyring that he had bought with the first rush of excitement at passing his test.

'Shall we go and get the tin?' She thought how babyish her voice sounded, more like four than fourteen. Out of her depth again. Then, like a kitten uncertainly touching a hedgehog she added, 'What do you think?'

Edward frowned as he turned the ignition key and seemed to be concentrating on the choke with an intensity that did not match the task. The engine started and Edward looked at her. 'Yes. Something's getting to her. I'll ask when I can have the car and we'll go. I'm not keen on the idea of not telling your dad.'

Caroline ignored the last bit. She felt fourteen again and relaxed as Edward negotiated traffic lights with boxes and the dual carriageway leading to their houses. No more was said. Both were anxious to return to normality. Homework, television, computers, all seemed blissful trivia after the nursing home.

'Thanks, Edward. See you.'

'I'll speak to you again,' said Edward nodding.

'And how's Aunt Clara?' said her mother appearing from the garden with a huge drum of slug pellets. She squinted at Caroline as she shaded her eyes against the sun. She brushed at her hair with a gesture that revealed how tired she was.

'She's fine. We had coffee with her in the lounge.'

'Oh . . . you must have stayed quite a bit then. Perhaps I need not bother going tonight.'

'Oh no. I shouldn't bother,' said Caroline sweetly. The aunt might have changed her mind. Caroline wanted to go for a ride with Edward and she wanted to nose around the cottage. 'You have a rest,' said Caroline. She watched relief make her mother look ten years younger.

'I'll have a night in then,' said her mother and wandered away scattering slug pellets, determined on mollusc genocide. Caroline opened her mouth to lecture her mother on the evil of slug pellets and the death of thrushes but then closed it again. She needed to keep a low profile till they had visited the cottage. Surely Aunt Clara had not really murdered someone . . . surely not? She had never married, been a librarian for half a century . . . but both Edward and she had felt the old woman's plea. Caroline tiptoed past her mother executing a snail under her shoe with a sound like munching crisps. She clenched her mouth shut and fled to the soothing chaos of her room and played CDs very loudly for an hour.

It was the following Friday before she saw Edward again. She was calling her cat Daisy when Edward called her name over the gap in the hedge. When they had been little the wide privet hedge had had a gap through which the children passed, a tunnel and a cave where plans could be made in private. The tunnel was now the territory of the cats but Edward and Caroline still found they met to talk by the old corridor under the bushes.

'Hi there,' said Edward his good-natured face grinning at her through the stems and twigs glittering with spring rain. 'I can use the car tomorrow afternoon. Do you still want to go?'

'You bet!' said Caroline and then kicked herself behind the thick hedge. She sounded like something out of Enid Blyton preparing for an adventure.

'I'll be round at your gate about one,' said Edward. 'It might be a bit later. Mum and Dad are doing Tesco or something first.'

Caroline nodded happily. Edward nodded and vanished. Caroline called the cat sweetly, in great contrast to her irritable yells of a minute ago. It looked like being a really good weekend.

She watched from the landing as some friends of her father's arrived for supper. Her lips curled as she watched her father smile. He never smiled at her any more like that. Well, it made her feel less guilty about what she had to do next. She waited for the sound of wine corks being pulled, heard the protest of chairs as middle-aged backsides crashed into them. She waited a bit longer until she heard the voices becoming louder, lubricated by Sainsbury's vino. Then she turned to the business in hand. The key.

Caroline scored a bull's-eye the first time. The key to the cottage was in an envelope in the drawer on her father's side of the bed. He'd even written on it to make her task easier. KEY TO WELL COTTAGE. Caroline took the key, pleased to see there was another identical one left. They were wrapped in four postcard sized rectangles of blue paper. Always curiouser than Daisy her cat Caroline had to look. She found they were weekly receipts for Aunt Clara's stay in the nursing home. £524-75p a week. Caroline stared. All that money for a week. She hastily strangled a feeling of sympathy for her father. No wonder he'd said, 'If she lives a long time in that place there'll be not even a brass farthing for you and me!'

Caroline tiptoed back to her own room, careful to avoid the creaking board on the landing that had betrayed night time trips down to the fridge when she had been little. Not that there was any need tonight. She heard a roar of laughter from below. They were probably telling the 'Jack's dead, Brenda' joke yet again.

'I'm going into Derbyshire with Edward for a ride. I don't know when I'll be back.' Caroline declared this statement to her parents like a declaration of war. But they said nothing. They had a large cafetière between them and were trying to eradicate the throb of drinking too much red wine. It was the first Caroline had seen of them. She had spent the morning trying different combinations of clothes for the ride. Now she watched with pleasure speculation, wonder, bewilderment pass over her father's pale face.

'See you.' She closed the door quietly and found Edward waiting, starting the engine as he saw her.

Very little was said as the city and suburbs were left behind. The moors were wide and open, still brown with winter. Now and again Caroline sneaked a look at Edward but he was intent on the road as it wound down to the river valley. They passed three ice cream vans and Caroline stared wistfully as they slid by. It was almost a relief when Caroline had to start to give Edward directions as they approached the picture postcard market town where Clara had lived for so long. 'Turn left here, Edward', and 'Half turn round the roundabout, up by the church and first on the left', all seemed passwords into a world that was under control again. Even so she could, like Clara, have killed. Killed for an ice cream, chocolate coated, full of iced mint fragments and morsels of fruit and—But Edward was smiling at her, at the triumph of a journey completed and a smooth entry into a parking space. Caroline dismissed the ice cream and smiled her thanks.

Well Cottage was the end one of three cottages that appeared to once have been a rather splendid Georgian house. A frilly fussy board, with WELL COTTAGE burned into the wood, was fastened to the wall with a tangle of wrought-iron flowers. It had been quite the thing in 1960. The middle cottage was now a boutique with a white dress in the window priced £399. WELL BOUTIQUE was scrawled in gold across the glass. There was a large board that announced PARKING FOR RESIDENTS AND CUSTOMERS ONLY.

'I'm afraid you can't park here. The shop is closed and this space is for residents only.'

Both Caroline and Edward turned to the voice and saw a woman waving her hands which were encased in yellow rubber gloves. She had popped out of her eighteenth century porch, a porch crammed with flowers like a zoo cage for plants. The woman waved her hands like an exotic insect and made haste round wooden tubs of flowers arranged as carefully as chess pieces. Caroline narrowed her eyes and scowled, her blue eyes icy with instant dislike.

'I'm Miss Walton's great-niece. We've come to collect come things for the old lady.'

The rubber gloves ceased their waving. Sly curiosity slid over the woman's features. She made a small sound, half disbelief and half assent and backed over the black and white tiles of her area. Caroline watched for a moment or two hoping she was filling the atmosphere with the hatred she felt. Then Caroline produced the key and prayed it would fit the door. It did fit the door which opened into Well Cottage with surprising ease.

'She's ringing someone. Your father, I bet.' Edward jingled his keyring. Coming from a tranquil household he feared the storms and stresses of the Waltons next door.

'Let her,' said Caroline. She never worried about the consequences when she was doing what she really wanted.

The dust fascinated them both. It was only the dust of months but already a fine moonlight of white dust shimmered on once highly polished furniture, lighting the air with the ghostly radiance of a first fall of snow. Caroline and Edward remained in the hall, uncertain. Caroline wondered if dust would settle like this in her bedroom. Her mother had raged last week that 'This is it, Caroline. I am *not* entering this *tip*, this *midden* of your room ever again until you clean it.' She saw Edward staring at a large black and white photograph.

It showed Clara, old it seemed in the 1960s, standing at the entrance to a large library in Manchester. Clara was standing with a very youthful Queen and teenage Prince Charles. Both Queen and Clara wore pearls. Next to it was another picture, Clara's retirement probably. She was clutching a tea-making machine.

'Look at her face, the old misery.' Caroline laughed very loudly. 'And, God. Look at that flared trouser suit she's wearing.'

Both of them laughed and the wintry atmosphere in the cottage was lightened. They went laughing up the wide staircase. The staircase seemed too big for the cottage and was uncarpeted polished oak. Caroline and Edward left footprints in the cold white dust in the cottage where old age and winter seemed to linger.

There were four large rooms upstairs and a tiny staircase that led to the attic. One of the bedrooms had been cut in half to make a bathroom. Caroline checked the bath for spiders and saw a blue dish with false teeth in it. The water had evaporated leaving the teeth stranded like a beached dead crab. She found the sight strangely depressing and hurried out into a bedroom. She turned the key of a wardrobe and yanked at the old door. The door opened and a fox's head on a long fur scarf leaped out at her and she screamed.

'It's this one,' shouted Edward. He had glanced out of the window when he had heard Caroline scream. The woman had finished phoning and was pretending to prune her plants. But she was watching Well Cottage, waiting to see what they brought out.

'Come on, Caroline. It's this one.' It was the voice he had used as a boy when he had found the best apples, the best tree to climb, the best bit of the stream to make a Tarzan swing. Caroline slammed the door on the fox and came at once. Edward had been quiet and smiling when he was a small boy—but the rest of the children on the road had always followed him, Caroline most of all.

The room was the largest bedroom of them all. It looked out to the graveyard of the church, everything now golden in the sun. Tourists sauntered with cameras and ice creams. A boy and girl sat holding hands on a nineteenth century vault. Caroline loathed the room at first sight. She imagined this room on a November evening with writhing trees and rattling windows, the tourists gone and the ghosts back in charge.

And this was a room fit for a ghost. The ancient chill communicated the fact there had been no heat or fire for years. Aunt Clara obviously had never used the room. You could sense that through the smell, the quietness, the still reproach of the objects in the room. Above all that it was a very masculine room in a Victorian way.

On a table was a blue and white jug and bowl, blue flowers on white pot with seven long and lethal cut-throat razors set out with a precision of pattern known only to Clara. All had black handles except the last which had a yellowish ivory handle blotched with some horrible ancient stain. The blades were as dull as old ice that had lain in a pond all winter long. But the sharpness of the blades beneath the dust sliced into the eye and made Caroline shiver a little. A top hat, straight out of a dressing-up box stood alone on another table. The silk of the hat was cratered with moth excavations and the dust gave the hat a cold moonlike appearance. Caroline was as still and silent as the hat.

Edward had picked up a heavy tarnished silver hairbrush and was trying it out on his hair but saying nothing. With the other hand he touched a pot-handled shaving brush with a plume of silver badger hair.

On the bedside table lay a gold pocket watch, a foggy sun in strata of dust-furred chain. A pair of gold cufflinks as big as dolls' mirrors lay by the gold-grey watch chain. Feeling her flesh pinch and wrinkle with fear, like crêpe paper, Caroline saw that there were boots by the side of the bed. Cracked and old with a network of cracks as fine as spider webs. Her eyes were pulled up to the bed. It was a room frozen in time, a room where an Edwardian man had just undressed and climbed into bed.

Then she saw the enormous black and white photograph, surrounded by a snake-thick ugly frame. A giant of a man sat on a chair, a man wearing the watch chain that coiled on the table as though he had placed it there. Then Caroline gave a half scream. God, the man was holding her hand when she was a little girl. Her head swam in a dizzy submersion into the waters of pure fear. When she surfaced she saw she had been mistaken. The man was holding the hand of a small girl. But the little girl was certainly not Caroline. It was Clara, there was no mistaking that, and Clara with a smile as big as the April sun. A smile that irradiated the tomb of the room. A smile of sheer delight as she half looked up at the great man. Written under the photograph in faded curly brown writing was EDWARD WALTON AND CLARA WALTON. Edward Walton. Edward, the name of the man she had said she had murdered.

A rattle of stones and a cry made her turn. Edward had his hand up the chimney. Caroline's hand that had flown to her mouth seconds ago to stifle horror now fluttered back again to stop a giggle escaping. Edward was clutching a tin and she helped him to his feet. His face was coated in soot.

'Well, there's her tin. Now where's the bathroom?'

While Edward washed in ice cold unheated water with soap as dry and cracked as old bones, Caroline examined the tin, wiped away soot and grime with lavatory paper. The grim bearded face of one of the Kings of England stared at her through the soot. She ran her finger round the edge of the tin and felt little beads like a rigid necklace.

'Sealing wax,' said Edward. 'So we'll not be able to look inside it.' He dried his hair and looked at Caroline. Nothing was said but each knew the other's thoughts.

Caroline followed Edward down the stairs drilling his back with a stare as hard as that of her ancestor on the bedroom wall. Never mind what he said. When she got home the first thing she was going to do was open that tin. She could stick the sealing wax back with Uhu. Aunt Clara was half blind anyway and she'd never know.

She slid on to the sun-warmed seat of the car and tried to dazzle Edward with a smile, a smile, though she was unaware of it, as brilliant as the small Clara's back in the grim bedroom.

'Let me buy you an ice cream, Edward, after all your hard driving.'

Five

Caroline's father was waiting by her gate, alert as a guard dog, face distorted with anger like a face in a funfair mirror. Caroline instinctively hid the greasy sooty tin under Edward's seat.

'Please, please, Edward, you keep it. Please, please—'

She could see Edward's honest and happy face cloud with consternation. Deception did not come easy to him. Caroline, who had battled with her father for years, was an expert. In fact Caroline now found she got an adrenalin buzz from situations like this. But with alarm she saw Edward faintly shake his head as the car slid to a standstill. She heard his keys jingle nervously as he saw the pure rage on Mr Walton's face. Caroline got out, eager to enter the swirling fury of the coming storm.

'Thanks a lot, Edward. It's been great.'

She saw Edward reach under his seat and grope. Her father shouted with a roar that was almost zoo-like in its frustration. He began to yell at Caroline. He completely ignored Edward, turned his back on him. Edward's fingers were round the tin but they let go. He shrugged his shoulders as though he were throwing Mr Walton off his back. He hated to be ignored. He certainly did not wish to be involved in one of the Waltons' whirlwind disputes. He put the car in gear and drove slowly into his own drive with the tin under the seat. When he got out he heard Caroline's and her father's voices volleying through the laburnums. He took the tin indoors and hastily shut the door on the war without. He took the tin to his room and quickly changed for badminton. The Waltons' voices hummed through the double glazing like wasps attacking an August picnic. He raced down the stairs, got in the car and drove to the sports centre thinking that his father was probably right when he had once said the next door neighbours needed a daily row in the same way as some people needed a daily vitamin pill. He could tell the last few minutes had only been a warm up. The big fight was just starting.

'Will you listen to me, Caroline. Will you shut up a minute. Mrs Parker rang me—'

'I've told you. So what? Nosy Parker rings you up. So what? Surprise surprise.'

'She rang me to say—'

'And I expect she's faxed and e-mailed the whole town, rung the *News of the World*, told the United Nations I've been to the cottage. Here.'

Edward saw Caroline throw her father a key as he passed their drive, saw her father lean against their car as if he was about to disintegrate and burn out with the white hot incandescence of fury. Caroline, nearer than the fleeing Edward, saw more. She saw fear in her father's eyes under the anger.

'What were you doing there?' His voice was strangled—a faint tremor lurking. 'Not that I'll ever get a straight answer from you. I went straight to the home when Mrs Parker rang. I got no sense from my aunt. She kept her eyes shut all the time I was there. Never said a word. She's had a non-speaking day, Dr White said. It happens sometimes in Parkinson's Disease. The doctor said she may not be able to talk to me for days.' His voice trailed as he took in air. Caroline imagined her aunt silent and with closed eyes as her father raged and she felt a spark of respect for the old lady. She watched her father inflate again, speak.

'Well, what were you doing?' The shouted question did not hide the fact he was almost afraid of the reply.

'Just getting Aunt Clara something.'

'What, for God's sake?'

'Nothing, as it happened.' She watched him carefully. Did his snarling face hope a little?

'My God, Caroline, you try me to the limit.' His shoulders slumped and he suddenly roughly shoved her in the direction of the kitchen. Inside Caroline stared in disgust at the kitchen. Fall out from the party still remained. Her mother sat at the big table with the wreckage of Saturday's *Times* and *Guardian* surrounding her. Caroline saw the jug of coffee, the aspirins. She was disgusted. It was the usual sad pattern. Her mother teaching all week, wine on Friday night, then the headache on Saturday.

Caroline gave a contemptuous hooting sniff. Her mother looked at her bleakly over those frightful reading glasses. She could hear her father muttering about her as he made totally ineffectual attempts to clear the chaos. He arranged discarded beakers into forlorn clusters of earthenware that looked like distant cooling towers of power stations. Caroline saw a thin lake of red wine advancing on a pile of unopened junk mail. And they called her untidy. Her father threw a wine bottle into the waste bin with a clang. His confidence was returning.

'What did she want you to look for? What did she send you for?' He spoke with mock patience, words spat out in unreal tolerance as though Caroline were an idiot.

'Something in a bedroom.' She saw alarm spread like a stain again on his face.

'What?' She saw the impatience was not just with her. He was on the edge of some precipice.

'She said we'd know it when we saw it.' Caroline lied with ease. Her father's unease fuelled her confidence. 'She was confused, the poor old thing. If I had my way—'

'Bloody hell, Caroline. Is that all you went for? Just an excuse to nose around? Mrs Parker saw you upstairs. I must say I'm surprised at Edward. Did you bring anything?' He was still on his guard.

'What should I have brought?'

'Did you go in all the rooms?' She saw how tense he'd become.

'If Mrs N. Parker says so we did.'

'And?'

'What do you want me to say?'

Her father began stacking plates by the dishwasher in clattering despair with his daughter. Knives hammered on the floor in a metallic hail.

'She's just confused. I think she just wanted us to see everything was all right.'

'She should have asked me.' She saw him visibly relax. He had been terrified about something. He opened the dishwasher and she saw he was now more bothered by the fact it had not been emptied than by her visit. Some jagged dangerous rock in the Walton Family waters had been avoided. Their uncertain ship had not been wrecked yet.

'Now, if you don't mind,' said Caroline, 'I've homework to do.' She turned to go but something in her father's mind ignited again erupting from some deep hidden well of volatile fear.

'Don't you ever go near that cottage again without my permission. There are some very valuable things in that house. Have you heard me, Caroline?'

'Yes. And so has half the town.' She was careful not to give him the promise that she would never go. She shut the door on the disgusting kitchen then stood by the door listening to hear what was said about her. But all she discerned was a nervous rattle of glasses being collected and a feeble request from her mother for more coffee.

Upstairs Caroline found herself edgy. She played CDs very loudly for an hour. She wondered about dust and how long it would take to settle in her room as it had in Well Cottage. As time went by she found her own mind relaxing as the dust settled there. There was more to Well Cottage than settling dust. Somewhere behind everything, silent as the white dust, powerful as a giant iceberg, deadening as a winter's day, was some force that had destroyed life.

'Caroline? Caroline?'

'What?'

She flounced off the bed to confront her mother, ghost grey with migraine, cradling a beaker of coffee. 'Please turn your music down, Caroline. I'm going to bed. I've had enough. You've done a wonderful job at upsetting your father. Something's made him unfit to be in the same room with anyone else.'

Caroline banged her bedroom door and heard her mother gasp as a thunderbolt of migraine tore through her body as an echo of the door slam.

It was the name Edward that bugged her all day Sunday. She could not settle to anything and her homework suffered for it. Edward Walton . . . Edward Walton . . . she had never heard the name before. She knew that if she asked her father it would be counterproductive. She sensed distress. She knew if she asked she would hear a version fit for a ten year old. Her father seemed anxious to keep her at that stage for ever, it seemed.

She watched for the next door Edward all day Sunday. She wanted that tin with her whole being. Happy to blunder and upset her parents she was acutely sensitive in her dealings with next door Edward. Certainly she knew better than to go round and knock on the back door as she had when she was six. Of course they would let her in, give her coffee, Edward would smile . . . but it would be wrong. You did not do things like that any more. Far better to see him by 'accident'.

All day she watched. She saw Robert delivering a free newspaper to all the houses and her face burned red with the recall. She wondered briefly why the word 'gay' may have triggered her aunt off. It seemed to have little to do with that chill cottage or a murder. At four o'clock she saw Edward emerge with his friend Lee—whom she hated. They were with Jennifer McIntosh and she hated her more.

Jennifer McIntosh put her in an evil mood and she did not speak during family tea. But passing her mother preparing her week's work she saw a family tree on a worksheet and she suddenly had an idea. When they were in the infants they had done a project on families and had taken a family tree to school. Her father had made her one.

Back in her room she commenced an archaeological dig. She dug deep through many layers of her past, down through artifacts containing signed photographs of desirable pop singers, down through animal refuges, saving the world from pollution, down and deeper until the Age of Dolls was arrived at. Two things delayed her quest. One was a plastic biodegradable carrier bag. It had degraded and the contents had spilled out long ago. She let the thin dusty strands of the bag trickle through her fingers. Fascinating. She also found a creme egg, possibly ten years old, shrunken, misted with mould and remarkably evil smelling. Beneath this stratum was the family tree.

As soon as she saw it disappointment settled on her like a cold breath. She recalled how disgusted she had been with her family tree. Other children had proudly turned up with hundreds of names dangling from complex TV aerial structures. Her own family tree had been a long, narrow, mean, withered line. True it had gone back quite a way. Abel Walton had married Lucy Prior when Queen Victoria was queen. Their son Jack had married Eliza Clay. They had had children. Ah! One of them was Clara, another was her own grandfather. Her grandfather had married Lily Gosling her grandmother. Both long dead or she could have done some questioning. Then came her father Jack who married Brenda. What a laugh. Then her, Caroline Walton.

She looked at the poor thing. It was incomplete. It had to be. People had millions of children in Victorian times. There was no birth control and children were always dying. She bet Abel and Lucy had had ever so many. Her father had lied to her all those years ago. It looked like a ladder rather than a family tree. Some kind of escape ladder for her father who was clearly escaping from a family secret.

By Monday night Caroline could stand the suspense no longer. Her father was at a meeting. Her mother had an open evening. She took a ball out to practise tennis determined to knock it into Edward's garden. She knew it was pathetic but she was desperate.

Six

Caroline volleyed the ball against the red bricks of the garage with a vigour more like squash than tennis. Her plan was to whack the ball, miss it, let it rocket over the privet into the old sandpit—where it would take help to find. Before this plan was complete she heard a jingle of keyring and turning saw Edward. Unsmiling but concentrating on her. The evening brightened. She saw him glance nervously in the direction of her own kitchen.

'Has Hurricane Jack blown himself out?'

Caroline giggled and explained. Then became suddenly subdued. Edward was still unsmiling. His usual good nature seemed to have drained away.

'I've been thinking. You know, about your aunt.' Caroline held her breath. All could be lost. 'Nobody has any right to tell her what to do or control what she asks others to do.' He was silent. It was a direct criticism of Caroline's father and he watched Caroline to see how she would take it. Caroline herself did not know what to do. It was a sort of unsaid taboo to make comments like this. Edward cleared his throat and she heard the car keyring shiver a little. 'I mean, if she wanted a tin from her own home she should have it. She might be ninety-three or whatever but . . . well . . . it's her tin . . . she's a right to be helped without all this grief.'

'Yes,' said Caroline. She felt like Colombus in mid-Atlantic, knowing where she wanted to go but clueless whether she was going the right way.

'I think we ought to take her the tin.'

Caroline resisted the temptation to throw her tennis racket high into the golden clouds of early evening, dance a wild line dance with invisible friends in the rhubarb patch. She tried to look solemn and adult. Put a heavy stone on the spring of happiness that was bubbling up in her.

'Yes . . . I think you're right . . . thanks, Edward.' She had a ten second silence for effect. Then, 'Nobody's going tonight. Dad's at a council meeting and Mum's at an open night at school . . . '

'We'll take the tin. I've got the car till nine. Your Aunt Clara has still got rights even though she's paralysed and living in a home.'

Caroline nodded, humbly, solemnly, thought about making a remark about what a good doctor Edward would make but bit the thought before it spoke.

'I'll just lock the door and put the alarm on.' She tried to walk slowly to the front door and appear deep in thought about Clara's rights. Instead she hugged an amazed cat indoors and sang as she set the burglar alarm.

Clara was in the lounge. Sunshine filled the big room, sunshine lit up Caroline's face. Clara was with two other old women, pretending to be asleep to avoid looking at the jumbo prints of endless grandchildren that another woman was passing round. The other old woman was knitting a baby cardigan, nodding politely as the jumbo prints kept obscuring her view of her lemon and pink creation.

'Hi, Miss Walton,' said Edward clutching the sooty tin.

'Hello,' said Caroline marvelling at Edward. Heı father must really have needled him.

'Wheel me to my room . . . please.' Clara gave the jumbo prints of the grandchildren a scorching glare.

'I was just showing your aunt my grandchildren. That's Diana. She's three. This is Tom, he's four. They've just got back from a very nice holiday in Greece and—'

'Some other time perhaps,' said Edward turning the

wheelchair with a hiss of tyres as though he had steered wheelchairs all his life. Caroline was again awestruck. She had always admired the manners of Edward's family, so different from the spiky minefield of her own.

It was cool and pleasant in Clara's room. The new young leaves outside the window made little moving sequins of light and shade on the floor.

'Here's your tin, Miss Walton,' said Edward. He'd obviously got a thing about giving her the tin but for quite different reasons to Caroline who was nearly exploding with curiosity.

'Can you get the sealing wax off for me,' said Clara leaning forward in her chair. Edward scratched the old sealing wax away. Nobody noticed the sooty greasy smudges on the bed they were using as a table. The lid came off and there was a silence.

Slowly the old woman leaned over the tin to get her damaged eyes as close as her paralysed bent body would allow. One hand was frozen still on a pillow, dead, white, still, like a cinema trailer for death. The other hand moved uncertainly towards the tin, a hand with a road map of blue veins and ugly red scabs from injections and drips. Both heard her breathing become louder, wilder. The living hand finally reached the tin and once there rested. Shining bumps from arthritic finger joints shone on her fingers like cruel jewellery.

Both Edward and Caroline were overcome by her powerlessness. Both had raged in the last years about the unfair world that seemed to control them. But their lack of control was nothing compared to this woman at the end of her life. And once the ruined hand had found the tin it was uncertain what to do. It scrabbled, clawed, rustled, but did nothing. One finger kept flicking and turning in senile repetition. Now Edward was at a loss. It was Caroline who saw the way.

'Shall I take the things out for you, Aunt?' Her voice sounded changed, a tape playback of a stranger.

'Yes.' Clara leaned back in the wheelchair and, horrified, they watched as she tried to control the shaking, the breathing, focus the misty eyes on the tin. 'Please.'

Right at the top was a newspaper article, dirty, yellow and faded, printed in tiny bold black print from the days of gas and candlelight. It was stuck to a piece of card with perforated stamp-edging, long before the days of Sellotape and instant glue. In larger print at the top Caroline saw the headline:

WALTON WILL HANG AT DERBY TOMORROW

Nothing in Caroline's life had prepared her for the reaction she felt. Possibly the sight of her own surname fastened to a death threat triggered it. Her stomach lurched with an Alton Towers roller coaster of horror. Then came waves of sickness cold as a hugging fog from a sunless winter ocean. Her hands shook like a premonition of her own inevitable old age.

With a great effort Clara leaned forward and with gasps, sighs, and groans shunted the grubby article along the sheets. She did the same with a soiled school report that Edward handed her from the tin. Caroline was paralysed by the sight of the headline. Nothing had prepared her for this. Under the report was a necklace of blue stones set in tarnished pinchbeck gold. Edward lifted the sky blue gemstones and placed them in Clara's hand where they rattled and chattered as she held them. Slanting sunlight rotated and twinkled as the necklace shook. Then the necklace escaped, trickled to the bed where it lay still.

Dumb with feelings she could not explain Caroline watched Edward hand Clara a black and white photograph, a postcard. The same man as the photograph in the desolate room in the cottage. But a difference. Here the man was smiling. It was a smiling photograph, a picture of a strikingly handsome man with a neat Edwardian moustache. A message in black ink had survived more than three quarters of a century. CLARA—WITH ALL MY LOVE, EDWARD WALTON. Then it fell to the bed with a flash of black and white like a single unlucky magpie.

Next a prayer book, plump, padded, self-assured Edwardian leather. A thin cross of gold gleamed on the cover like lines of sunlight showing through curtains in a darkened room. The aunt dropped it at once. The book seemed to burn her hand so quickly was it released.

'Edward gave it me,' whispered Clara. They heard her breathe in and out, four, five, six, maybe seven times. Noisy breathing, the body quivering with Parkinson's Disease. Then, 'It says in there I shall burn in Hell for what I did.'

Caroline saw the distress and forgot her own. But was at a loss. Her mother and father were cheerful atheists—boasted at parties about it. Caroline had no compass to steer her aunt through her last storm. She hadn't a clue what it might say in the prayer book. She leaned forward however, sure of one thing—that there was no such thing as the Victorian idea of Hell where devils toasted victims on the prongs of long forks.

'You won't go to Hell. Nobody believes that now.' She wasn't too sure about it but a look from Edward suggested she had done the right thing. And the look from Clara was the look of someone who has just been rescued from a burning building. Clara blinked, silent with the shock of rescue.

'Read that to me.' She clearly meant the newspaper article. 'Please.' Caroline, now more able to cope, reached for the article. She saw it had been stuck to a piece of card from the lid of an ancient shoe box. GIRLS' SANDALS

NAVY BLUE 9/11$\frac{3}{4}$d. Caroline's mind wondered for a moment but it was as meaningless as the prayer book.

'Go on then. Read it.' There was the Clara she knew of old. 'Read it, then. I can't see it now. Don't ever get old.' This last to Edward. 'Read it now.' Caroline took a breath fearful of what she might read. 'Please.'

'Edward Walton of Moonfields Farm, One Ash, Derbyshire, will be hanged at Derby Gaol for the brutal murder of one of his farm labourers. Readers will recall that Walton, sentenced at Derby Assizes a month ago, was also associated with other sinful dealings that this paper, a respectable family paper, would not dare to name. Readers will not have forgotten how Walton attacked and then burned—'

A woman in white, smooth and sleek in white nylon overall, entered the room with a trolley as big as her smile. From this she took a clipboard and widened her smile by another two teeth.

'Hello, Clara sweetheart. Would you like any sweets or magazines?'

'No.' A look that would shrivel a soldier in an asbestos suit.

'It's the day for Curly the hairdresser to come in tomorrow. Will you be having a perm, Clara?'

'No.' Clara heaved in her chair and looked as if she could pick up her bed and attack.

'Would you like a peek at next week's menu? There's your favourite farmhouse roly-poly on Thursday with, wait for it, home-made raspberry jam. Sounds delicious, doesn't it?'

'No.' The room was packed with hostilities like a chocolate box of ground-glass creams. Hostility, anger, fear, disgust.

'I won't stay then, Clara. I can see you're a busy girl tonight.' Invisible poisoned darts launched from Clara's clouded blue eyes. The trolley whispered away, the cool white professional armour of the woman still as smooth and as unchipped as a white sugared almond. A long, long silence. Then Clara surfaced from the deeps of her helpless rage. Breathless.

'Nobody *ever* called me Clara. Not the girls under me in my library at Manchester. Just Mum and Dad . . . my brothers . . . and Edward.'

Still very breathless. 'Water, please.' Edward held the ugly beaker that was designed not to drip. Clara made a wry face at the tepid water. Caroline, shaking a little herself, guessed the problem, took the beaker and ran the water in the wash basin till it was cold from underground pipes chilled still by February's frosts. She filled the dreary coloured beaker and carefully cradled it in the shaking bent hand—the one that still attempted to deal with life.

Clara drank and Caroline yanked tissues fiercely to mop the water that still escaped from the half paralysed mouth.

'I can't begin to tell you how I hate it here.' Neither Edward nor Caroline could cope with this headline statement of despair. They heard the breathing become a little slower. 'Lift me up a little . . . please.' Glad to do something that prevented them reacting to the plea of hatred, they both pulled Clara up in her chair. 'Now go on . . . read . . . please.'

' . . . attacked and burned alive his labourer in the cottage close by the farm. Our faithful readers will, of course, remember Mr Justice Sparrow donning the Black Cap in his courtroom with these words to the savage animal that we must conclude Walton is. "You killed your labourer with evil calculation and a vile intent that beggars the belief of this Court. After you have been hanged by the neck in some other place, as I have just sentenced you, you will meet your Maker with blood, murder, fire, and unnatural sins on your hands. Yet I believe it was your sudden violent loss of temper that brought about your downfall and for it you shall die."' Caroline hesitated, choked, suddenly feeling a stranger in her own family. 'Full report on pages three, seven, and eight.' She let the card fall in her lap.

This was an emotional Hiroshima to Caroline. Fragments of thought fluttered about her brain. Would she pass these criminal genes to her own children? So, there had been a criminal in her family. How much did her father know? But what was Clara going on about killing these men? How could she? The hanging and the murder had nothing to do with her. She must only have been a girl when all this happened. Poor Clara. The teasing at school. And what was the present day Edward thinking? About her? Her family? Were they mad? Was she mad? She looked up at him under her eyelashes and saw his face as unreadable as stone. Then she saw Clara, pale as a living corpse fighting with words that seemed to be internally strangling her.

Edward leaned forward and gave her the plastic beaker again. His own reaction scared him a little. His first reaction had been flippant. He had wanted to say to Caroline, 'Well, the Walton temper's still alive and kicking in your father.' But that was something he never said to Caroline then or at any time in the future. Then he felt a surprising surge of rage at the old woman's helplessness. Obviously she needed to sort problems out. And she was reduced to talking about it to strangers. It made him angry. He did not know why.

'I tried to stop thinking how I killed them . . . get on with my own life . . . forget what I'd done . . . I hid all his presents in that tin . . . hid it away . . . tried to live . . . my life . . . what an evil little thing I was . . . my life . . . ' She became incoherent, fragments of a lifetime's thinking, like broken links of a long chain, falling into the room. Then there was a silence. The silence grew. Caroline began to fidget, sort the tin out. She saw rings, grubby silk flowers, a tiny gold watch, thought they looked more like lovers' gifts than anything else. The silence became menacing. Embarrassing.

'You'll have to take me there . . . out into Derbyshire . . . To the old farm . . . by ourselves . . . don't tell your father . . . I want to tell you everything I know . . . can't stand it any longer . . . you take me out . . . '

'Yes,' said Edward briskly. 'We'll get you there somehow if that's what you want.'

'And if they will that's the best thing I could prescribe,' said a warm southern Irish voice from the bottom of the bed. Turning they saw a smiling young doctor and a nurse with a trolley crammed with medicines. All three had been enclosed in a time capsule from the long past. They had not heard the entrance of the doctor.

'It's the happy hour, Miss Walton. We've brought your cocktails.' Smiles. Caroline felt there was sunshine in the world again, loved the doctor second only to Edward. Clara did not smile. She was now past all that, but neither did she try to mow the doctor down with newly sharpened glares. She lay inert while swabs were dabbed, injections eased in, then swallowed an endless assortment of pills and syrups as obediently as a sleepy toddler. The doctor finally signed some paper as the nurse gave Clara something out of a tiny chest with a strong lock on it. Then he turned to Edward and Caroline.

'If you can cope, a trip to wherever she wants to go would be great. Talk to Sister here.' He gave the nurse an acknowledging smile as she watched Clara drink something that had come from the closed box. 'You'll need a variety of pills and possibly one of you will have to give an injection if you're out for long. You'll need a wheelchair. A catheter. Sister will explain if you're willing. 'Twon't be easy but you're the ones to do it.' He twinkled at Caroline who would have done anything to please.

'We'll manage,' said Edward, shortly, almost rudely. Still handling feelings he did not know he had.

'Edward can give the injection. He's going to be a doctor.' Caroline babbling with shock from the earlier revelations, then wishing she could cut her tongue out and bury it for ever in the Clinical Waste bin at the bottom of Sister's trolley. Felt a child of seven. A fool. Went as red as the syrup dregs in the base of Clara's medicine glass.

'Your father's dead, Caroline.' A sleepy Clara, eyes dilated with powerful medicines, was being adeptly slid into bed by Sister.

Caroline looked helplessly at the doctor.

'Gently but firmly say no,' said the doctor. 'She's asleep now. Your aunt is receiving very powerful medication for the pain for her arthritis and cancer. Sometimes she becomes very confused. Says she's killed people. Or she has fantasies, says she was going to be a doctor before she murdered somebody. All drug induced nonsense which you must gently say is not true. Miss Walton has led a blameless life as a librarian. She used to be a great hiker, a walker. To take her out into the Derbyshire hills would be a kindness and a tonic, bless you both.'

Edward picked up the tin, collected the grubby litter of the past from the white bed. Caroline saw Clara suddenly open her eyes, swim to the present, saw her focus on herself, was convinced she saw a look of cunning flicker over the pale old face. Then the expression altered, closed with the habit of a lifetime of never revealing her feelings.

'Will the weekend be OK?' said Edward in the car, his only words.

'Yes,' half whispered Caroline.

'She's probably talking rubbish anyway,' said Caroline getting out of the car several traffic lights later.

'She's every right to go, whatever she's talking,' said Edward. Snappish. Superior.

'Yes,' said Caroline feeling as tall as the wheel hubs as she climbed out and obediently absorbed Edward's suggested times for meeting on the following Saturday. Hoped and prayed that this was the weekend her father was going on a course. Then going up the drive half hoped her father would not be going on a course and they would not be able to go. Everything had got out of hand. She wished she could go into a nunnery for three weeks to think. Just think.

'Darling, you've been to see Aunt Clara again?' Her mother on an adrenalin high in the kitchen, full of parents' compliments on her GCSE classes. Caroline stared at the make-up her mother now only wore for school open evenings. Thought about a remark about Joan Collins but then decided she wanted to think her own thoughts. In silence.

'I've just ground some fresh coffee. Would you like a cup?'

'Yes,' said Caroline. 'Please.'

Seven

During the week Caroline lost weight like a snow-woman waning in hot gusts of acute anxiety. Never before had she felt life so unstable, her whole life seemed to be melting away underneath her. For one who had begun to thrive on family chaos she now found herself nostalgic for a quiet life now vanishing for ever.

On Sunday night she realized Edward had the tin and hated him for a macho pig, taking charge of her family secrets. Then loved him for taking care of it. After all, she had arrived back from the nursing home traumatized and the tin completely forgotten. Then she hated him for taking charge.

She saw Edward on Monday night as she fetched washing in from the garden, washing three times soaked and dried by weather her mother simply had not observed. She heard the irritating jangle of Edward's keys as he got ready to drive to the sports centre. Saw with alarm her father returning from work, white and grim, hand as pale as marble round a bundle of files. Her breath was sucked in for fear Edward would say something combustible to her tense father. She loved him when he shouted, 'Good evening, Mr Walton,' dropped a rain-grey tea towel in the mud when he shouted, 'See you Saturday, Caroline. About nine OK? We need an early start.' Back inside she knew she could not cope any more.

' . . . had one hell of a day. Now I've got to go and see Clara. God, I am fed up.'

Caroline tiptoed away. She could not begin to think of excuses for taking Clara out on Saturday. Her tracksuit bottoms felt as if she had taken the wrong waist size to the fitting room.

Thursday teatime. Tracksuit bottoms now two sizes too large. Coming slowly down the stairs in a personal fog of anxiety, Caroline had gripped both tracksuit and knickers in a tense clench, fearful both would plummet to her ankles. She stared at the pitifully thin pizza, framed with black owing to her mother's misreading of the cooking instructions. Saw her father pick his up and snap it with a crack as he shot a look at her mother blissfully munching and reading the *TLS*.

'You haven't forgotten, Brenda, I'm going on that damned management course this weekend, have you? It was on the Year Planner but that looks as if you've let it fall down the back of the fridge.'

For the first time for centuries Caroline wanted to run round the table and hug him. That was one problem solved. She managed to eat four mouthfuls of the hardboard with the aid of a lettuce leaf until the anorexia of anxiety closed down her digestive system yet again. What if the doctor said something to her father? Or the nurse? Was it all worth it anyway? The more she thought about it the more she wondered if Clara had made it all up, this killing business. Her great-great-uncle, or whatever he had been, had been hanged and the other man burned. So what had Clara done? What was she babbling about?

'I can't eat any more of this.'

'Thank you,' said her father eyeballing her as if she was six.

'Thank you,' said Caroline cramming as much hatred, sarcasm, and contempt into the word as she could. She slammed out and rummaged in her coat in the cloakroom. She found a Mars bar she had bought on Monday and could not tackle. She ate it now with silent savagery outside in the hall, felt better and just a little in control of everything again.

All that remained was to see her father off on Friday evening. Returning from school Caroline hovered, wasplike, round the kitchen, unable to settle. She was rewarded by a typical aggressive early arrival of her father.

'God, Brenda, I am pig sick of life. I shall have to go down to the home and see Clara. She wasn't too good last night. Just stared at me through half closed eyes. Then I'll have to make a mad dash for York if I'm to be there for eight. Can you remember when we last went out to the cinema, or even the pub together?'

Nobody replied. He began to eat his meal standing up by an oasis of space in the kitchen. Caroline's mother sat in a chair by the big window drugged with anticipation of the coming weekend. Caroline fluttered in a corner pretending to make a salad, holding her breath until her father went. Would hold her breath until she was certain her father's tired eyes were steering their way up the M1. She was terrified a doctor or a nurse would mention the trip out tomorrow. She studied her father over a bag of salad she was half-heartedly opening. He *is* dead, she thought. Poor man. Clara was right. She held the salad aloft while she analysed with interest and alarm this sudden new feeling for her father. She stayed like this until her father departed in a whirlwind mix of stress and disorganization blended with spurts of fiery temper.

Now for the worst bit. The next half hour. She expected the phone to ring and her father's voice ranting, 'Christ, Caroline, what the hell are you playing at taking the aunt out tomorrow?' She stood biting her nails while her eyes did a tour of the kitchen and her mind slipped into Hate Mother Mode, a mode that always soothed. The visual tour of the kitchen began with the radiators where huge black V-shaped fangs of toasted tights and leggings hung stiffly. Her mother's laundry. Then she looked at the picture rail where, she counted, were eleven unironed shirts of her father's. Idle old fool, she thought, earlier sympathy evaporating with the heat of her sneer. But the shirts, stiff and white relics of her father, made her uneasy. He was going to ring. She could feel the phone holding its breath.

Caroline's nervous frantic eye travelled to the kitchen floor. Ten huge bags of flour, bought for the cottage in France, bought because they were on offer somewhere. One had already burst, the bottom one. The cat had made paw prints in it that even a blind Sherlock Holmes could spot. Don't let the phone ring. Her eyes darted to the coffee beakers on a windowsill, silent monuments to Wednesday's oversleeping. By them was a dishcloth, sculpted to a grey lily with a putrid heart. Don't let it ring. Her eyes flew to her mother still immobile in the window. The inspectors at her school had called her mother the most successful language teacher in the county. Boy, they should see her dishcloths.

Back from her mother Caroline absorbed the olympic rings where hot objects had stood on surfaces. Was that a bath towel *and* a bra entwined over the oven door? She studied an oil slick by a gas ring, mentally photographed a bottle of olive oil skating with some balsamic vinegar in a secluded corner behind an empty cornflake packet. The table cloth, littered with school books, was stained with red wine like a map of the old British Empire. Next door's kitchen, Edward's kitchen, was not like this. Surfaces free, fresh flowers, the scent of newly baked bread and coffee. Both Edward's parents worked in sweet partnership. Don't let it ring. Please.

She turned, not at the phone, but a baby piglet snore. Her mother had collapsed in a vale of cushions, mouth open, a glass of red wine tilted, about to spill with Archimedean certainty. A new hardback novel crashed to the floor. Her mother's hand sleepily dithered over a crisp bag. How I hate her, thought Caroline. Then she was aware of the grandfather clock in the hall announcing the hour. She was safe! She had to be. She approached her mother smiling grimly.

'Mother? . . . Mother? . . . Mother!'

A vibration buzzed from her mother's lips, a hybrid of a snore and sigh.

'Mother, I'll go tomorrow and see Aunt Clara. Give you a rest.'

'Oh, Caroline, could you, darling? Would you?' Caroline saw a mask of youth fasten itself to her mother's face with a relieved smile. Then her mother became servile. Creeping. Fawning. Caroline's Hateometer registered very high.

'Yes. I don't mind. Edward will give me a lift there.' She left her mother abruptly. Her mother sipped red wine, ecstatic at the thought of a day to herself.

Edward was waiting next morning. She could sense his determination as steely as an east wind. Little was said. May sunshine illuminated the big lounge of the home. Clara was bright, waiting in her wheelchair. Tried a crooked smile with the half paralysed mouth. A very old lady perched on the piano stool of the grand piano with a handbag, almost as big as she was, played 'Land of Hope and Glory'. An old man conducted this with a rolled-up magazine. A beaming nurse appeared and Clara was whispered away with a purr of wheelchair tyres.

Both doctor and nurse explaining. Edward ferociously intent, the expression he had when he played squash. The nurse smiling and talking to Caroline.

'This is the catheter bag. It's fastened to her leg. It will collect her urine. So you need not worry about taking Clara to a toilet unless the bag gets full. Then you will empty it down a toilet bowl and get a fresh bag.'

Horror, revulsion, despair, embarrassment, all four clouted Caroline. Horror mostly. She took the fresh empty bag in its sterile package and was dumb.

She could not cope. Never in her wildest worries had she

expected this. Aghast she felt a tide of blush flow into her face. The nurse continued, brisk and matter of fact.

'This is Clara's calliper. Watch me put it on. It's easy. She doesn't need it in the car but in the wheelchair it *must* support her paralysed leg. Otherwise the foot will turn and pull and tear muscles. Can you buckle it now?'

Red with bewilderment, face aflame with ten kilowatts of heat, Caroline buckled two cold steel fasteners. Now the Irish doctor was charming Edward and nurse was smiling too. Caroline was left clutching the dreadful cold plastic monstrous bag.

'Right. You're over eighteen so you take this diamorphine.' He handed Edward a bottle of innocent raspberry-red liquid. Colour of baby medicines. 'One of these spoonfuls if the pain begins. No more than one every hour. We must have the bottle back.' Caroline felt mutinous. Edward had the easy bit. Then she changed her mind. The doctor handed Edward a syringe.

'Clara *must* have her insulin at one o'clock with or without any food. But she must eat between twelve and two. A meat sandwich would be ideal. *No sugar.* She can have an ice cream or a sweet biscuit in the middle of the morning.'

Caroline clutched her bag and watched helplessly as the doctor let Edward practise injecting a bean bag. Both doctor and Edward looked pleased with themselves. I shall throw up, thought Caroline. And meant it.

'One last problem.' Speaking to both of them now, although Caroline was too sick and faint to care. 'I've given Clara quite a large dose of dopamine to stop the shakes from her Parkinson's disease. Clara will begin to shake a bit as the day goes on but she should be fine for the morning. I want her to enjoy today. For a woman who has been used to walking all her life, walking the hills, being in a wheelchair must be agony. The problem is the dose of dopamine I've given her might just cause hallucinations. She may imagine things from her past. But at least she will be alert and her head will be still so she can look around and see the things she once loved.'

The nurse was breathless with writing instructions and handed them to Edward. Caroline, now pale and full of dread about the bag, was disregarded.

'To the car then,' said the nurse. 'Lovely sun,' she said to Clara as they processed outside, Caroline forlornly at the rear, miserable with the catheter bag. She clutched it hopelessly while the nurse and Edward slid Clara on to the back seat.

Silence. Edward was concentrating on the traffic, heavy traffic all on its way in May sunshine to the Peak District National Park. Caroline, terrified of changing the bag; Clara peering, narrowing her eyes, desperate to recognize hills and moors she had lived with for ninety years and now kept away from. They approached the picture postcard market town, the inevitable traffic crawl, then jam. Excited blurred talk from behind them.

'See! See! Up there on the hill. My grandfather's farm. Your great-great-grandfather, Caroline. Edward was born there, grew up there. Edward used to tell me ghost stories. The place was haunted by a monster that lived under a standing stone—'

'Really?' said Edward with his middle class interest absorbed from his parents. But Caroline was deaf to family history. What if the bag burst now? Spilled in Edward's car? They'd no towels or anything. And she hadn't a clue how the vile thing worked. The nurse had explained but, oh God, she couldn't remember what to do . . . Caroline was wrapped, encased in an armour of worry. She hardly heard the aunt babbling away. The car stationary at the roundabout in the market town.

' . . . and Edward bought me those blue beads you saw in the tin here. I was the happiest girl in the land . . . '

'I shall never get the bloody tubes back in if the bag comes off,' Caroline muttered miserably. Edward tutted as a blue car swerved in front of them. A six mile climb to the limestone hill country. Sunshine on Clara's face. The twisted smile again.

'It used to take us two hours coming back up here from market. On this hill Edward walked with the pony while Rose and I stayed in the cart.'

'Who was Rose?' Caroline's voice was as irritable as her father's, worn out with worry about that dreadful bag.

'Edward's housekeeper.'

'Oh.' Caroline wanted to turn to see if the bag was all right. Prayed it was not full. Her nails dug into her palms, then she plucked at a mole on her neck, a childish trick that used to worry and annoy her father. Then she squeezed her lips with anxiety till she tasted blood.

'We'll begin by the school. That's where the story begins.' Edward steered for the village car park. Caroline said nothing. 'Please.'

Edward was determined to get the last parking space on the village street. Got it. Smiled at Caroline, who did not smile back. Then they installed Clara in her wheelchair, or at least Edward did. Caroline was still helpless with worry over burst and leaking bags. Trippers who had come to see the picturesque village and its duckpond and tea room found much interest in a very old woman, stiff as a stick, being slipped into a wheelchair by a tall good-looking young man and teenage girl angry, flushed, sulky, very red in the face. Clara suddenly laughed as Caroline, redder every passing second, shook and struggled with the cold steel of the calliper. The laugh was cracked, a laugh little used for more than eighty years. Caroline stood upright and glowered at the little staring crowd. There were a few people as old as Clara in the audience, faces as bland as watching babies. The crowd moved slowly away to other attractions as Caroline peppered them with scalding stares.

But the village school where Clara once had been, amazingly, a child, was a school no longer. Gold letters swirled on a varnished blackboard above the door: THE OLD SCHOOLROOM—Afternoon teas. Coffees. Edward said nothing but wheeled Clara across the playground now packed with parked cars. Halfway across Clara's shawl became entangled in a wheel and Clara's progress came to a jerking halt. Caroline wriggled it, tugged at it, felt like crying. A man with a baby came across and smiled. He handed Caroline the baby and unravelled the shawl. Caroline held the sleeping child and marvelled at what was happening. She tried to see the level in the catheter bag. She gave the man one of her rare and genuine smiles as they carried on.

'We'll have coffee in there.' Clara was back to her old self. Edward made a face at Caroline, shrugged his shoulders, grinned. He pushed at the churchlike door but holding the wheelchair could not move it. Caroline stepped forward, pushed. The door swung open and a pot plant fell from an old milking stool and crashed to the floor. Edward wheeled Clara inside.

A floral print rocket of a woman exploded from the chintz within. She picked up the plant and looked at Clara and the wheelchair as if they were bringers of plague.

'So sorry,' said Caroline using a tone of voice that caused spluttering anger when she directed it to her father. Caroline felt suddenly better. The nightmare bag forgotten. Here was someone to battle against. Someone to blame for a very strange Saturday. Edward had selected a table and was steering Clara with as much care as he steered his father's car.

'No. Not there.' The woman was snappishly triumphant, out to revenge the pot plant, eager to regain power. 'That's reserved for luncheon.' She made traffic police actions to a table behind a dresser groaning with souvenirs and flavoured teas. Caroline at once scented the flavour of discrimination against the disabled. As did Edward.

'If we're in the way or unwelcome please say so,' said Edward. Caroline blinked at how well Edward could mimic his father. 'My friend in the chair wants a seat by the window. She was at school here once.'

'Three filter coffees, please,' said Caroline, pleased to be on the winning side. The coffee came and they sipped it, Clara drinking with her good hand hardly shaking. But of stories of murder there was no sign. Not even the beginning as Clara had promised. The bill came. £4.50. Hell, thought Caroline, digging with despair in her pockets.

'I'd like a lollipop,' said Clara suddenly. It was clear her thoughts at the moment were far from stories of murder. She pointed to a freezer chest draped with a lace shawl in a vain attempt at Heritage. Edward swirled the chair towards it. The floral proprietress put her hands on her hips and stared. Caroline did the same and the woman looked away and another waitress gave Clara the lolly of her choice, an ice construction that hinted at mutated raspberry, or a space rocket, depending on personal perception. Edward scanned the label, scanned the nurse's notes, paid for it, and Clara ate it. Clara was the ten year old again, the child who had come to this school, the child with the long forgotten laugh, the echo of which they had heard in the car park. The lollipop half gone, a trickle of meltwater from the paralysed side of her mouth, then a torrent of speech.

'This used to be the top class. I sat here. I was top of the class. Dr Mossley, the vicar, you know, used to come into school. He studied wild flowers. One morning, just like this, he brought a bunch into this room, forty different flowers. He wrote the names we used on the boards and by their side the Latin names. Next time he came in, he said, he would give a silver threepence to any child who could remember three of the Latin names. At the end of the day the teacher, Miss Gibbs, rubbed them off. Next week when he came back I could remember all forty names. He gave me half a crown. He said I must sit the scholarship for the High School in Buxton. He said I was clever enough to go to one of the women's colleges at Oxford. I could be a doctor he said. He had great expectations of me. But then I killed Edward, you see, and my life went wrong.'

Boring, said Caroline inside herself. Caroline's mind, like a microwave on high voltage, cooked and processed thoughts. Was she making it all up? Were these drugs she had for medication making her say all this? Was this a wasted Saturday? Then Clara held the half finished lollipop out like a discarded toy. Caroline took it and scrunched the remains. Her filling sang and throbbed in her top tooth. Caroline saw a trickle of red juice reappear down Clara's chin and was overwhelmed with tear-pricking pity. If she hadn't got a story, well, she'd had a day out. She dabbed at the carmine thread.

Edward wheeled her out of the now silent café.

'Fancy bringing such a poor old sick creature like that in here.' Caroline turned, sneered at the room with lollipop red lips, devastated them all with one red glance. Going through the entrance the wheelchair nudged an old blackboard no longer listed with wild flowers but announcing DERBYSHIRE FARMHOUSE SOUP WITH GARLIC & LENTILS. The board swayed, crashed.

'Leave it,' ordered Caroline, dictatorial as her father. 'Leave it.' She raised her voice. 'BECAUSE WE'RE TOO BUSY SEEING TO A SICK OLD CREATURE TO PICK IT UP.'

Unexpected laughter from Clara again. The laugh more sure of itself, a long forgotten merry bubbling spring. It infected Edward and Caroline as they steered through the shimmering heat of parked cars in the old yard. They were still laughing when they paused by a golden sun-warmed gatepost that was carved deeply with GIRLS ONLY. Edward was the first to straighten his face and body. He was still proving something to himself.

'Where would you like us to take you now?'

'Up the big hill where it all started,' said Clara, coughing and cackling into Kleenex. 'Please.'

Eight

Caroline felt invigorated again, in charge, practical.

'What about our dinner, sandwiches or something? Didn't Dr O'Connor say Clara must have a sandwich with protein or something?' She was glad to be one step ahead of Edward in medical matters. 'And we shall need a drink to help the medicines go down.'

'There's Jim's Bakery.' Two hours of normal life and Clara was interacting and talking, her face taut, younger, the drooping mouth firmer. Edward, with a soft jingle of his precious car keys, crossed the village green causing slight turbulence to Clara as her head turned to see familiar sights. And Jim, when they got there, was as old as Clara, wrinkled peachstone of a smiling face floured in the creases.

'Well, by gum, I'll go to me Aunt Nora's. It's Clara Walton.'

'I've come to take a last look round. The farm . . . you know . . . everything.' Clara raised her good hand, perhaps in greeting, perhaps to hold back faces and memories from her youth. At her words the old man appeared flustered, disturbed, a little red under the flour dust and white hair of old age.

'Aye . . . we'll mek it to one hundred, thee and me, Clara . . . Aye. Tha'll find big changes since . . . ' The old man could not produce the appropriate words for what had happened. 'Aye. Tha'll be wanting grub if th'art traipsin' up that hill.' With that he vanished leaving all three of them uncertain what to say.

He returned with sandwiches after five minutes, with the supreme confidence of old age, certain in its knowledge that it knows what is best for everyone. Without being asked what they wanted Caroline and Edward were handed two weighty ploughman sandwiches bursting with the unripe, creamy crumbling cheese of central Derbyshire and spring onions from the garden. Clara's bag contained elegant triangles of brown bread containing tongue and ham with tiny lettuce leaves and mustard. Fastened to the top of Clara's bag with a rubber band was a bunch of lilies of the valley straight from the garden. The air was throbbing with unsaid thoughts mixing with the scent of the damp lilies.

'God bless,' said the old man. Clara and Jim stared at each other. A tear squeezed out of Clara's undamaged eye, one from Jim's pale blue eye as though each were a mirror image. Caroline's five pound note was waved aside. Caroline herself was seized by a floury hand, and stared at from Jim's face and white hairs.

'God bless you, pet, for bringing her. She's had a tragic life. I was in same class over at school with her. Cleverest girl in the school. Eh, I did want her for my sweetheart, all them curls and them big eyes. Aye. School didn't finish till four and she used to be frit of going up that hill in dark. Used to let me kiss her under railway bridge if I walked the two miles back to where she lived. Then . . . aye . . . well, never thee mind. It's all water under bridge now. Then she went to Manchester, worked in a library. Used to see her at weekends hiking round the hills. Wrote a book about Dove Dale for Manchester Libraries. Gave me a copy. But 'er were never the same after what happened. Aye. Tha' reminds me of 'er before all the bother.'

He patted her hand and Caroline felt like she did when she looked at her grandfather's *Times* crossword. Clues that meant something at once to her mother's father were meaningless to her.

'This way then,' said Clara as Caroline emerged from the bakery, sharp at being kept waiting. Caroline and Clara sharpened Walton stares on each other, then the sun came out from behind a cloud.

'You don't know how good it is to be out in the fresh air . . . the sun. It's lovely.' Neither Caroline nor Edward replied but sensed genuine pleasure.

The empty road that Clara had once trudged in the grey ghost light of January afternoons was empty no longer. Bored families stared from a line of slow-moving cars. There was no pavement. The hill was steep, exhaust fumes dried their throats and noses. The sun created archery targets of sweat and dust and heat on their T-shirts. Nobody spoke. It was half an hour, longer perhaps, before the road widened, the traffic flowed and they could sense the silence of the countryside shyly edging back. Another twenty minutes and they were in front of a restored farmhouse, now a second home or a holiday home. Black and gold gates guarded four-wheel drive vehicles. A huge white sign indicated that this desirable fortification was called MONKSBARN.

'What does that say?'

'Monksbarn,' said Caroline wearily. Edward put the brake on the wheelchair and sat on a stone platform that had once been intended for milk churns. Aerobics with the chair had drenched him in sweat.

'Well, the name's the same. This is where I used to live. You'll soon know why I've brought you all this way.'

Then silence save for the sudden whizz and streak of a car, the barking of a dog inside the suspicious watching house. Caroline felt her breathing settle. Felt the sweat cool and go cold. Did not expect what the aunt said next.

'I hated my mother and father. I loathed them.' Clara's words were stinging, brutal as wasps. 'I hated them with every fibre of my body.' Edward looked at her with a professional eye of concern. She was breathless with long imprisoned venom. 'When I used to live here the place was no better than a pig sty. Piles of cow and pig muck all over where those jeeps are parked. Or whatever they are. Rusty old buckets, nettles as tall as I was. Old pans and broken pots my mother had just thrown out of the back door. I was the oldest, you know. Mother couldn't cope. Used to drink gin from a lemonade bottle, tell me it was lemonade. There used to be a big clear glass marble in the bottle that clinked as she drank. When I think of her kitchen . . . buckets of sour stinking nappies, damp washing all over. And my father—your great-grandfather—no better than a pig. Never washing unless you can call grunting at the pump on a Sunday morning washing.'

Caroline found herself shocked to hear Aunt Clara talk of her parents like this. Felt a faint sense of disgust in the way she did when her parents' middle-aged friends discussed sex. It felt as if something had slipped in the order of the world. It was very right and proper for Caroline to carp and criticize her mother and father . . . but to hear Clara rant in such a way was . . . inappropriate. She stared.

'And I refused to help. Would not lift a finger. And why should I? My father and mother had made all the mess, made all the children. If they chose to live worse than the animals in the farmyard it was no concern of mine. Lord, I hated, *hated* the very sight of them. I used to run away for hours on end. My father took off his belt and flayed my legs. But I would not do anything. He used to hit me and I used to stare back at him. Just look daggers at him then run off again.'

Edward was smiling faintly, perhaps embarrassed, perhaps making secret comparisons in Walton family history. Caroline watched her aunt, lips pursed, more Victorian than her aunt. The old woman was now on an adrenalin high of ancient hatred. Both eyes in stern focus on the past. Her good hand was clenched to a fisted salute to an unrepented battle eighty-five years ago.

'Yes. I used to break my neck to get out of that stinking hole. I used to run out of that gate, right up the hill to my father's brother at the next farm. Edward. My Uncle Edward.'

The name choked her, suddenly the rage died. Silence. A car passed changing gear audibly. A woman came out of the house of old hatreds and watered a hanging basket that now hung on the pump above the restored cobbles. It was an excuse to stare at the curious trio that had halted before her gate. Nobody heeded her. Clara was now sailing down some current of the past known only to her. Edward rattled his keys. Caroline wondered at the strange depths of her own family's history.

'Edward.' Clara whispered the word. Relished it yet breathed a sadness into it that chilled the May sunlight. Five cars sped by. The owner of the restored farmhouse went in and slammed the door.

'Uncle Edward. He lived at the farm further up the hill. I want to go there. I want you to help me sort things out.' She settled back in her chair. 'Please.'

Edward pushed the chair again finding energy from a vague sense of all the things he hated in the world—particularly bossy, overbearing men like Caroline's father.

Under an elegant three-arched disused railway viaduct Clara spoke to nobody in particular. 'When I reached here I used to stand in the middle of the road and stick my tongue out at my father if he was looking.'

Edward laughed. Caroline did not, wearing the expression of Jove when his thunder had been stolen.

Nine

It was a long hard road to the farm, and the May sunshine had developed a harsh glitter. They took it in turns to push the chair. Two conversations provided intervals as they climbed uphill. Caroline, trailing while it was Edward's turn, wondered at a small wood, vivid as a restored oil painting, fistfuls of young ashleaves green cut-glass against the enamel blue of the sky. A thrush, blackbird, chaffinch, wren, and a chiff-chaff made a quintet of birdsong with a stream as harpsichord continuo. The wood was crammed with bluebells, moonpenny daisies and a red flower she did not recognize. She picked the red flower and showed it to Clara when she and Edward changed over the pushing.

'Red Campion. *Melandrium dioicium,*' announced the aunt after holding the vivid pink flower almost to grazing point to her good eye.

Caroline retained the picture of the small wood in her mind as she pushed the chair ever upwards. It was like some pictures in holiday brochures, too good to be real. The tiny flower-filled wood contrasted with the endless green fields, stone walls, and merciless sun. Clara suddenly spoke, eerily echoing Caroline's private thoughts.

'The flowers have gone. There used to be flowers in the fields and all along the roadsides. Now all I can see is green. I can't see even a glimmer of colour. At this time of year I would pick bunches and bunches for Edward and Rose and Dr Mossley. And for school. And to put in my dump of a bedroom. Now they've gone. Have they gone?'

'Yes,' said Caroline. 'They seem to have all gone.' A few buttercups round a tree, moonpennies here and there: for a time this replaced darker thoughts until once more Edward was forced to rest after a long haul. Across a field was a large Georgian farmhouse basking in the May sunshine in front of a protecting belt, a belt of acid green sycamore trees.

'That's it. I can't see it properly now but I know it. That's where I used to escape the pigs at home.' She paused, gasping a little. Edward's eye checked her out before she went on. 'I only used to come up the road if it was wet and mucky in the fields. Usually I'd run across the fields and under the railway.' She waved and directed their stare to a diminutive tunnel under the railway bank where black and white cows were solemnly processing. Caroline shaded her eyes to look at the disused railway, now a heritage walk where hikers, like worker ants, followed the fingerposts.

'There was peace and order at Moonfields. My Uncle Edward and Rose the housekeeper understood me. Let me stay. They knew what Monksbarn was like, the dirt . . . Our garden was full of dung and cabbages and elder and broken plates my mother chucked out. At Moonfields there was a walled garden. Like walking into a huge jewel box. Everything tidy. Everything in its place. Beds of mint, sage, horseradish, and roses everywhere you looked. And inside scrubbed floors and blazing bright fires and the smell of bread and roasting meat and woodsmoke. Pans hanging on the wall like mirrors. And of course Uncle Edward. I loved that man too much . . . so much more than the pathetic brutes down the road back home . . . '

Caroline and Edward made no response at all to the aunt's passionate speech. They were out of their depth on this voyage into Edwardian England.

'Everything Uncle Edward touched turned to gold. Everything my father touched turned to muck. Hard to believe they were brothers. What are those bees skimming along the railway line?'

'They're motor cyclists in yellow jackets following the old railway,' explained Edward.

Another long pause followed, all three of them contemplating the past. No cars whisked by. A plane high above nosing down for Manchester Airport could be seen but not heard. A lark rose. Caroline and Edward were curiously aware of a past countryside, now a ghost, a past world with Clara as its last link, a link soon to break.

'Edward was almost a gentleman farmer. He wore a top hat.' Edward tried to catch Caroline's eye to exchange a grin but Caroline was chilled by the sense of old miseries. 'My father wore a filthy smock, sacks on his shoulders on wet days.' She turned to Caroline, perhaps sensing increased awareness. 'My father only shaved on Sundays. Rose brought Edward a clean starched shirt every morning with a jug of hot water to wash and shave with. You'll have to lift me over that gate.'

Caroline and Edward stared foolishly and helplessly at a gate. A tiny fingerpost announced PUBLIC FOOTPATH TO ONE ASH over a lilliputian stile designed for the under fives. Barbed wire was looped everywhere along the walls—Stalin and Hitler could not have arranged it better. The gate had a padlock as big as a small pumpkin, leaden fruit not to be touched.

'If she wants, over we'll go,' said Edward.

'Let's eat first,' said Caroline suddenly violent and ravenous with the tension. There was an ash tree by the gate with mottled shade, a trough with amber veins of sunlight reflections. Clara ate her delicate sandwiches at once as though such a picnic happened every day. Edward administered the tablets, injection, and diamorphine with a slickness that shamed Caroline. She plucked up courage and took a deep breath. She made herself check the catheter bag. Thanked silently any god who might be listening that it was half full. She wiped her hands, feeling almost professional, on a clinical wipe provided by the nurse. Feeling a little happier she took out the considerable sandwich.

'You see, you'll have to lift me over the gate because that path leads to where I did it.'

Caroline's appetite died. She tried to tell herself it was the medicine talking. She wanted to think the old lady was talking rubbish but in her innermost being she knew this was not the case. Instead she sipped mineral water while foreboding breathed its icy breath upon her. Edward demolished the bread mound, ruthless as a bulldozer. Clara ate the triangles of brown bread, turning the morsels over and over as she did so, seeming to greatly enjoy herself. Caroline found herself in suspense, sick at heart, waiting for what might be revealed next, but very thankful for the catheter.

A car approached. Stopped on the other side of the road. A man got out. A woman. A young boy and girl. A very small toddler.

'Family with 2.4 children,' said Edward behind the half demolished ploughman. Caroline giggled despite her sense of impending doom. The family, spotting Caroline's picnic party, had sensed this was the spot for picnics and imitated their choice. Edward watched from behind his bread as the father took out a white disc from the car and screwed on four legs. The mother wriggled at a mass of plastic like an incompetent magician and suddenly, hey presto, had four white chairs. A salt and pepper pot was placed exactly in the middle of the table. Plates, knives, and forks were solemnly arranged. The family sat down and slices of pizza were handed round. Caroline did not know whether to laugh or scream. The family were so still and watchful that Caroline wondered if they had fallen out of the sky. The only movement was pizza approaching solemn mouths and the handing round of the golf-ball salt and pepper pots. Cans of drink appeared. Clara seemed splendidly unaware of the alien invasion.

'Lift me over, then. I'm ready . . . Please.'

The family watched attentively, silently, quiet as if they were viewing television in their own lounge, thoughtfully chewing, as Edward and Caroline lifted Clara on to a bank of daisies. Clara as light as a doll, weight stolen by cancer.

Caroline squeezed through the hostile stile. She was glad that the stress of the last week had thinned her thighs. Edward folded the wheelchair with authoritative clicks and snaps accompanied by the percussion of his keyring. He passed the chair over the gate. Two cans being opened at the intense family picnic hissed their approval. Edward gently lifted the featherweight Clara as easily as plucking a daisy. A cake box sighed appreciation from the picnic as the family opened a Sara Lee Gateau cold from Iceland. Caroline received the burden of Clara over the gate, staggered, drew in a breath as she thought of the catheter strapped to Clara's leg. She saw the neat threat of the barbed wire tinselling the gate and trembled at the thought of punctures. Edward, nimble as a shadow, was through the stile and together they installed a breathless Clara in her wheelchair. The family, sensing it was time to switch channels, switched on Radio Derby on the car radio.

'I'll bring the video camera next time. I'll make a feature film. Let you enjoy us in the comfort of your own home,' shouted Caroline to the family as Edward began to push the wheelchair. The family, sipping coffee from plastic cups, stared back, passive as grazing cows. Edward made a noise. It was hard to tell if it was approval or amusement. He thought of remarking about the Walton temper but thinking about it kept quiet.

Silence again except for the hiss and murmur of wheelchair tyres on the baked mud of the lane, and suddenly a plangent chord as a pebble from the old packman's trail hit the spokes of the wheels. Two blackbirds sang a conversation about their personal territories. The faint drone of a plane high in the blue faintly reached their ears. One skylark descendant of the thousands that once sang above the untidy pastures of Clara's father exulted invisibly directly above them. Always the way led upwards towards the blue edge of the sky and the unknown.

'Stop!'

Greatly alarmed Edward stopped pushing. Caroline rushed forward. But there was no medical emergency. They had reached their destination. Edward turned the chair so that the aunt faced the big farmhouse below them, three fields away. Caroline saw her aunt was shaking slightly. The demon of the Parkinson's disease was winning again as the doctor had said it would. Clara's hand was vibrating like a leaf in a faint breeze. And Clara's face was contorted in horror and misery.

Edward arranged the rug over Clara's knees. They were on one of the highest points in the district. A short path led to a Camping Barn designed to shelter campers from the worst of Derbyshire weather. A hawthorn bush faked snow with its blossoms above them wrapping them in its disturbing fragrance of almonds and sweet fish. But Caroline saw none of this. She saw only Edward as he arranged the rug, checked the brake, and gave Clara a plastic glass of mineral water that trembled with tiny tidal waves. Caroline knew everything Clara had said was true. It was not medicine that was going to talk. It was the past.

Edward leaned against the limestone wall, warm in the sunlight. He genuinely felt he had achieved something worthwhile. Clara was wriggling a little, making herself comfortable, looking down to her beloved Moonfields. All a blur now but memory focusing the gentle farming scene. But Caroline stood, sick at heart, a great foreboding in her mind.

Ten

Clara licked her lips and with a tremor in her voice began to unburden herself.

'One day—the lilacs were out, I know that—a tramp called at Moonfields. Knocked at the door. There was nothing unusual in that in those days. Tramps walked the main road from Buxton to Derby Workhouses, seeking work. This man had been a soldier in the War, so he said. Asked for a job at Moonfields. Nothing strange in that either. Tramps often did. It looked like a place to settle down in, you see. It looked like home at last. Edward gave the man a job as labourer, let him use this cottage.'

She turned, with considerable effort, to peer at the Camping Barn. Her hand, shaking with Parkinson's and emotion, directed their gaze to the barn. At the end of the Camping Barn it was possible to guess that there had once been a dwelling. A gritstone door frame was filled in with red brick, as were the two window frames—one at ground level, the other above it.

'Are the gritstone lintels scarred by fire?' Clara's voice sounded suddenly weak and alarmingly vulnerable.

Edward screwed his eyes in the bright sun. He presumed her precise reference library language meant a door frame.

'Yes.'

Clara jerked her head away and gasped at the pain of the movement. She looked into the past and Moonfields, was silent for a very long time. She began talking in a hushed voice. So quiet that the blackbird and the single lark plaited their talk into Clara's.

'Suddenly Edward stopped noticing me. This new labourer turned out to be a marvellous singer. He had a rich deep powerful baritone singing voice. That was something to have in those days, you see. We had no television or radios or record players even. Anyway, Edward bought a brand new piano for the south parlour at Moonfields. He organized musical evenings. My uncle had a good bass voice, was leader of the village church choir. The church organist used to come up to Moonfields and play the piano for the two men and they would sing. Hymns, religious songs, music hall songs, opera, Gilbert and Sullivan. It was quite something to hear them sing the duet from *The Pearl Fishers.*'

Suddenly she stopped. Her eyes became fixed and staring. Two young cyclists raced along the old railway track below, shouting, ringing their bells, laughing. Vanished round a curve. A cow mooed sadly. The lark, now high and invisible, poured down song on them. Edward looked professionally at Clara. Caroline touched the good hand, finding herself afraid of death for the first time in her life. Then Clara drifted back from some Edwardian nightmare, blinked. Wondered who the young man and woman were. She blinked a few times and focused on the modern world, remembering who they were.

'Yes. My uncle had musical evenings at the farm.' Her tone had become wary, clipped and politely formal. Clara struggled to shrug off the cloak of suffocating pretence she had worn for eighty years or more. She managed to struggle out like a battered butterfly in November sun, too late for summer. She was shaking more violently than before.

'I was *so* jealous . . . I'd longed and longed for piano lessons and he had not bought me a piano. Everyone wanted lessons then. It was the thing. I asked him if I could use the piano and would he pay for the lessons. I don't think he even heard me . . . '

The hand became greatly agitated, shaking as though it conducted some tragic overture from the past. Caroline took it and held it like a quivering bird in her own. She found that she could not bear to see the shaking hand any longer.

'My uncle did not see me any more . . . no more trips to Bakewell Market, money for books, beads, and necklaces, or fancy chocolates just for me, his special girl . . . the light had gone from my sky. He had been the only thing in my life that had been rock solid, organized, wholesome, clean. Now he was a stranger to me. Jealous . . . oh, my good Lord, was I jealous of this man who sang and charmed the whole village. I think if I could have found a dagger I would have stabbed him. I knew all about daggers from reading the *Arabian Nights.* My uncle had given me half a crown and I had bought it from Bakewell and read every story.'

Another long, long painful silence. This time they were ready and accepted it. Clara's journey to the past had many tunnels. The lark descended and was silent.

'One day, hating the world, hiding from the world, I was up in the hay loft at Moonfields. Even my uncle's hay was superior to ours. Light, fragrant, packed with dried flowers. My father made dusty musty rubbish. I was stuffing myself with liquorice and sherbets to stop the misery. Down in the yard was the corn shed and I could see through the window. Everything sparkled at Moonfields, harness, corn bins, window glass. Through the glass I saw Edward and the man touch hands and smile at each other. I guessed the rest.'

A chill wind, a wind with the ghost of winter in it blew the creamy blossomed boughs above them. The blackbird ceased in mid sentence. Clara looked Caroline full in the face.

'We were not as innocent as some people think we were in those days. I liked school. I used to join in games with the older boys in the school yard. I was good at just about everything before . . . Well, I'd heard about things some men and boys did. But I'd thought nothing of it till that moment in the hayloft . . . '

A shoal of cloudlets dimmed the sun. Above them the blossom hardened to ivory, hard as the colour of winter. Phantom winds of old winters whispered round the barn.

'Are you warm enough, Miss Walton?' Edward, polite and caring.

'I've not finished talking yet.' Clara tumbled back into her fortress of waspish retorts that had guarded her whole life. She saw the hurt expression on the young man's face. 'Thank you.' She vaguely discerned she had been rude and ungracious. 'I'll be all right thank you.

'But this man . . . this tramp . . . was a devil . . . a monster . . . the sort they warn children about in schools nowadays . . . Weeks and weeks later I'd run away from home. It was late one June evening. Sun still in the sky at nine. The last night of peace in this world for me. I'd refused to help my mother clear up the mess she'd made during the day. My father had threatened to take his belt to me and thrash me. So out I'd run. Not to Moonfields any more. Instead up to Uncle Edward's hayfields. All high and ready for mowing. All crammed with flowers and seeding grasses like a magic carpet. Walking in the fields before mowing was not allowed but I did not care. I walked, made paths, flattened the grass to punish Uncle Edward for not loving me any more. I knew the men with their scythes would not be able to cut the grass I'd flattened. As I wandered about I picked orchids and flowers for school the next day, to give to Dr Mossley. The tramp saw me. I was quite near here.'

Another silence. The sun sailed from the little rocks of the clouds but the light seemed colder, remote. Looking at the National Park landscape, neat, tidy, it reminded Caroline of a neatly tended cemetery, the farms tombstones to lives long past.

'He said he had some chocolate and would I like some. Chocolate was a rarity then. A real treat. I was past caring about anything then. Greedy for chocolate which was a comfort of sorts. I followed him into the cottage. The one behind us all bricked up. He asked me for my bunch of flowers. I gave them to him. Plenty more outside for the picking. I saw he had a bruise on his face and found I was glad. It looked as if somebody had hit him really hard. I was glad. Perhaps I smiled. Perhaps he thought I was smiling at him. Anyway, he touched me. Some of the village boys had tried to do that and I would not have it. He laughed at me. I told you, children are warned against people like that these days. He was a monster that would have done anything for his own ends . . .

'Then he said I could have all the chocolate I wanted if I was good. He turned to the cupboard that was on the wall there, I think he was going to show me the chocolate. Well, on the table was an axe he used for firewood. And all my misery, jealousy, hatred for this man, for life, my mother, my father, my dirty farm, all boiled up and over, like the red froth when Rose the housekeeper made strawberry jam. I hit the man with the axe. Knocked him out, I think. He fell, gripping a cloth on the table where his clay pipe was smoking. The cloth fell on top of him . . . Well, I ran for my life as fast as I could. Got in my bedroom from the scullery roof as I always did and saw in the distance this cottage on fire. I remember sitting on my bed watching it blaze away and eventually saw the tiny figures from Moonfields trying to put it out.'

Around them the May landscape was as quiet as winter. Only the wind blew softly in the white branches above and round the smudges of black on the Camping Barn.

'Weeks and weeks went by. Nothing happened. I said not a word. Everyone thought the tramp had run away. The night I had hit him he had had a fight with Edward. Edward had hit him, knocked him to the ground. The man had been snaring rabbits in a field of grass, treading it down, spoiling it for the mowers. Edward hated anything going wrong in his fields. He was a perfectionist. So they thought the man had run away, set fire to the cottage for spite and cleared out.'

Clara stopped and gave a moan that took your breath away. 'Oh . . . the pain . . . ' Caroline watched as Edward measured the diamorphine in a tiny plastic glass, the liquid blood-red and outlandish in the green and white farmland. Edward watched as keenly as he watched his A Level chemistry experiments. But Caroline watched cold and helpless. She suddenly sensed Clara transferring a huge burden for her to carry. She sensed it would be as great as that of Atlas.

'Just give her a few minutes,' said Edward briefly. He was very much in control of himself and Clara. Caroline hated his guts again. He perhaps dimly felt that and plunged his hand in his pocket and fiddled with his keyring. Caroline looked away from him, angry at she knew not what. She saw her aunt's head fall forward as though she had fallen into deep sleep. All she could do was to hold the hand that still trembled with some kind of life.

Edward got to his feet abruptly. After a time Caroline recognized sounds from Edward and realized that he was smoking a cigarette. So arrived another shock to Caroline's world order. She realized she knew nothing about anybody, her aunt and her feelings, or Edward's. Caroline suddenly felt a Victorian aunt herself, critical of Edward's response to Clara's murder confession. And critical of Clara's raw childhood feelings of hate and jealousy and anger. Up to that moment Caroline had assumed she was the only one in the world who felt anything at all.

Eleven

Clara was immobile, head on chest, for twenty long minutes. Whether she dozed or waited for the pain to ebb neither Caroline or Edward asked. When finally she did speak, freed for a time from the octopus stranglehold of pains it was with a slower voice. Parkinson's, banished for such a short while by medicine, was now sneaking back like frost after brief winter sunshine.

'But I thought—I thought you said—You said you had killed two men. Killed them both,' said Caroline, stuttering, stumbling, clumsy. Now she had no straws to cling to after that chilling confession. Caroline discovered her voice sounded thin, childish, like a petulant five year old begging for a story to be complete. Clara ignored her.

'Well, September came. I had passed the scholarship to go to the High School in Buxton. A free place. But I needed the uniform and a great deal else besides. Uncle Edward paid for the lot, hats, blazers, hockey stick, books . . . he paid. But he was a changed man. I was no fool. Though he bought me everything for the Cavendish School, I knew, I sensed he was missing that devil I had . . . that was buried under the rubble of the burned cottage.'

Another of the silences that old age seemed to drift into, except this one was welcomed by Edward and Caroline. They both needed time to weigh the immense confession and measure out their sympathy. It was like seeing an Everest of a mountain loom out of cold fog, an Everest where you had thought there was a hill. To begin a new school, go every day knowing there was the body of someone you had killed back home. Edward took a deep breath of fresh air. The cigarette had not helped.

'Wasn't there anyone . . . I mean anyone who you could . . . you know . . . tell?'

Edward was ignored as Caroline had been. The journey back to the past left Edward and Caroline as marginalized as two children waving to an express train. Already Clara was miles away, far ahead. This journey would not stop until the terminus.

'It was a wet September. The wettest they could remember down in the village. Every morning I would walk up to the station with my new satchel, with my new Swan fountain pen and my new pencil case and my new school mackintosh and new hat. And it meant nothing. I was dead from fear and the horror of what I had done. The other girls would laugh and joke and do their homework on the train but I would not talk. I used to press my nose on the cold glass and look up here at the burned cottage and wish I was dead. The other girls called me Lady Snooty. Uncle Edward had bought me everything even the richest girls had. But they did not have what I carried around with me.'

'But surely, Miss Walton, there was—'

But the train thundered on. Again he was left standing.

'It was a wet September. The wettest they could remember down in the village.'

God, thought Caroline, now she's started to repeat herself. But Clara knew the route precisely. It had been travelled over with herself for company every day for over eighty years. Sometimes three or four times a day—or more.

'Storms blew in every day from the Staffordshire moorlands, drenching rain and low clouds. Drenching thunder showers brewed high on Axe Edge and washed away the harvest. Rain lashed and washed away the debris of the cottage. The roof had fallen but wind and rain began to slowly work at the ruin. And someone saw a bit of the body.'

Edward and Caroline stared. It was the kind of story you knew would get worse but prayed against the odds it would not.

'Uncle Edward was arrested soon afterwards for the murder of the farm labourer. They were convinced he had done it. You see he had had a fight with the labourer before I . . . before I had done what I did. Edward had hit the man in temper and chased him out of the farmyard. The shepherd had heard him say "I'll kill you if you go on my mowing fields again". And worse for my uncle someone from the village had said Edward and the man were lovers. Now in those times you could be put in prison for years doing hard labour for being gay, as you all call it now. If you were gay you were thought to be sick in the mind and body. So you see the police had no difficulty in arresting my uncle. There was a witness to say he had threatened the labourer. And they thought he was a sick man because he was gay. He was arrested and . . . '

Caroline and Edward perceived it was the stage of the journey when there is no going back. It was nearly over. This was the time to reach for safety belts, grit the teeth, lean forward a little.

'I was too terrified to speak. If I had said I had murdered the man they would have locked me up—'

Caroline made a protest but Parkinson was conquered and Caroline was brushed aside with a push of the hand.

'Oh, they would in those days. At worst I would have hanged. It did happen and I was of an age when this could have happened. At best I would have been locked away in Bakewell Workhouse with girls who had had babies or been violent. With the rough home I had they would have just taken me away in a locked horse-drawn van. So, I stopped living when I was twelve years old. I scraped through Cavendish, too knotted up to work properly. I just managed to get a job in a library in Manchester. The girls at school called me Snooty to the end of my time there. Dr Mossley was very disappointed with me. He had been convinced I was destined for Oxford or Cambridge . . . But my life was ruined. At sixteen I began to learn to escape into books . . . That's how I've lived my life.'

'Couldn't you have talked to this Dr Mossley? Wasn't he a vicar or something?'

'Good heavens no. He would have been shocked to his foundations. He was on the Board of Guardians of the Workhouse. I would have been sent there as a violent or insane patient.' She looked at them as though they were strangers. Which they were to her world of strict morals and certainties. She spoke again in a distant voice, a great distance away.

'Will I burn in Hell, do you think? Dr Mossley would have certainly said I would.'

'No.' Synchronized denial from both Edward and Caroline. Their heads were shaken in a small line dance of denial. It was curious that they were both so certain. Caroline's parents had no religion, had been known to mock and despair at places where religion caused bother in the world. Caroline had early absorbed the idea religion was a nuisance. Edward's mother went to some church, his father now and again, but drops of religious belief had rolled off Edward's back like water off a duck.

'But . . . ' Clara whispered from a world away. 'But . . . not only did I kill Edward by keeping quiet, I loved him too much. It says in the Prayer Book you may not marry your uncle. I used to tell my brothers before . . . before . . . that when I grew up I would marry Edward. So there's another reason to go to Hell.'

'No.' Amazing certainty from Edward and Caroline, united in a powerful shout. Then silence after the thunderclap of the word. Both were soaking in the deluge of horror. The enormity of it all. One life ended by a stupid, selfish lunge at a young girl. Another brutally destroyed by the noose of hanging. And a twelve year old left with no understandable life. And the ghost of that twelve year old staring out of Clara's face begging for comfort and understanding. Old as Clara was she still had the faith of a child that someone will make it better.

High above them the wind roughly shook the hawthorn boughs. Petals fell like snow and stayed on the paralysed hand. Clara was unaware of them. Instead she peered at Caroline and Edward like a child viewing the world from a prison window. Her good hand seemed to brush away invisible cobwebs from her sight.

'I couldn't speak. My mother and father would not have listened. In any case they were so ashamed of what had happened. As soon as Edward was taken to Derby jail and the business of him being gay was known, the duke's men came and put his furniture out on to the road. Rose the housekeeper was sent packing. I saw all this. And said nothing.'

More petals fell. It was the beginning of the end for the brief fragile blooms. Some petals fell on Clara's hair, some on the scalp where her hair was thin.

'You young people talk so freely now. Nearly all the flowers and birds have gone, but you can talk. That gives you freedom. I'm beginning to feel alive again . . . but it's too late.'

Caroline said nothing.

'So I said nothing. And let Edward hang.'

A blizzard of hawthorn petals distorted the view of Moonfields. Far below a boy laughed as the wind blew his cap away over the walls of the cycle track on the disused railway. Clara's hand felt burning hot as Caroline took it again.

'They took Edward's farm away from him at once. He only rented it from the duke. My uncle and Moonfields, the lovely Moonfields, were lost for ever. But he had been a good farmer. Had made a mint of money. He had bought fields and woods round Moonfields. When the railway was being built he supplied the navvy camp with food. And his mother—my grandmother—Grandmother Walton—loved him the best of her six sons. Mind you, I was scared to death of her. She looked like you do, Caroline, when you're mad, like you were in the School Room this morning.

'Grandmother Walton had given Edward Well Cottage when she died. And when Edward was hanged and the Will was read, Uncle Edward had left everything, Well Cottage, fields, woods, money in the bank, all to me. There was some for Rose as well. So you see I've been one of the richest, unhappiest women in twentieth-century Derbyshire.'

Then a Niagara of tears. Years of suppression cascaded out. The torrents shook Clara's frail body. Two hikers walked by, caught Caroline's Grandmother Walton eye and pretended there was nothing unusual about an old woman crying her eyes out while two young people sat by her side. No end to the fall of tears and blossom. It was Edward who eventually moved.

'I think time's nearly up, Miss Walton,' he said gently. 'The doctor said you would need medication before tea.'

Clara managed a remarkably childlike smile behind the tears. The unsophisticated smile of the twelve year old left behind years ago. Caroline began to mop up with Kleenex. She was astonished at the quantity of salt water and briefly thought of Alice floating in on her own tears. Then slowly they set off together, saying nothing but keeping close by each other.

Twelve

The journey of a lifetime was over. The long day was finished and the sun was already touching the tips of the woodland on the west side of the nursing home. The grandfather clock in the lounge watched their arrival through the window, impassionately ticking away the seconds. Caroline, numb with emotional exhaustion, vaguely thought of an aircraft, damaged, in distress after a long-haul flight. For as soon as the car stopped and Edward opened his door, nurses sped out to the tarmac, rapid as airport firefighters. Smiles flashed as dazzling as the westering sun. Professional gushings, soothings, and careful handling bore Clara away.

And Clara, half asleep now, drowsy, her thoughts still in a faraway land never to be seen again. Eyes unfocused she seemed to be talking to the golden sun that now cast the shadows of the higher leaves on her face.

'Thank you . . . ' Her voice distant, tiny, like a long-distance radio signal. Then vaguely to the sky, 'I've had a . . . nice time.'

'If that was a nice time tell me about a bad time,' muttered Edward more to himself than anybody. A nurse, now in charge of the wheelchair, heard him.

'It's been a day out with ordinary people.'

Edward and Caroline followed at a distance, both silent with anticlimax. Caroline looked at the paper sculpture masks of faces that inhabited the home, masks that expertly hid the lifetimes of the wearers. An old man with giant false teeth and Buddy Holly glasses, a 1953 silk cravat covering a worn out neck, stared into space. His fingers drummed a rhythm that welled out of some deep private cavern of his ancient mind. As Clara whistled by at emergency service speed he did not move an eyeball. He, like Clara, had a faraway land of eighty years making.

Caroline began to sweat, wanted to run from the emergency exit that was wide open to the world as they passed. She wanted to flee these padlocked faces, from a past life that had been passed to her, deep as a poisonous shadowed well. She wanted to rush round to her friend Liz and gossip maliciously about schoolfriends. She wanted to buy ten Kinder Surprise eggs, wolf down the chocolate and make the tiny models, and leave the empty capsules on the floor to enrage her mother. She wanted to lie on her unmade bed, wrap herself in her quilt and peep out and watch *Neighbours.* She needed to stuff her mouth as tight as a cushion with salt and vinegar crisps. She needed to go down to the bus shelter at nine o'clock, just as it was getting dark and see who was there. Anything to escape life and lives.

And for a few hours she managed to refuse to hold the parcel from the past that Clara had so deftly handed her. She fell asleep at eleven and was oblivious to the world until three in the morning when she awoke with a suddenness that racked her whole body.

She had not been dreaming, she knew that. She also knew that she was no longer alone in the room. Her mouth was desert dry, too clogged to scream. She switched on her bedside light which revealed nothing but the squalor and chaos of her room, empty of human presence. Yet the feeling did not leave her; she could sense her father's presence, hostile, critical, ready to punish her. She could sense Clara, her guilt and lifelong misery seeping into the room like venom from a dying reptile. Most oddly of all she could feel a stare. The stare from Grandmother Walton, Clara's grandmother. It was this stare that prevented sleep for two hours.

When light began to sweeten the atmosphere in the room Caroline could not calculate where the fear had come from. Part of her felt it had blossomed like flowers of evil from within her, like ancient dreams passed on. Yet she also sensed that the fear was outside her and she had been visited by the past. She was so unsettled that she sat next to her mother at breakfast time and ate a bowl of All Bran hoping it would purge her of mysterious feelings. Her mother had not brushed her hair and tents of the Sunday papers she had flicked through surrounded her. Caroline briefly thought she looked like a very dirty old hippie in a camp at Glastonbury but said nothing. She ate the cereal and examined these new sensations and thoughts.

The nightmare without pictures kept her from dwelling on her father's return and his possible discovery that they had taken Clara out. So immersed was she in trying to navigate the black waters of the experience and at the same time do her maths, French, and history homework that she was almost surprised to see her father erupt into the kitchen. She had drifted through the day dazed by the experience and now it was evening.

Ice-cold arctic fear washed away the hot dark fears of the nightmare. Irregular verbs fled like swallows as winter approached. He knew. She could see that. He sat down heavily at the table, his face as contorted as a winter seascape. He savagely thrust a pile of exercise books along the table, and the consequent shunting of debris caused an empty wine bottle to roll off and continue to roll under the table. Caroline held her breath, frightened as though she was four. The bottle stopped rolling. She heard his angry breathing. Found she had pushed on her fibre tip so hard the point had disappeared.

'I've just called in at the nursing home, Brenda. Aunt's in some sort of a coma. Mind you she looks peaceful and happy. It's the drugs they give her, I suppose . . . Doctor says she's sinking . . .'

His face writhed with sudden temper. Caroline stood up.

'Matron says she had Taylor the solicitor in this morning to make a new Will. Before she slipped into this coma. Now why the hell did she do that?' He shunted the books again and a lump of cheese, half wrapped, the remains of her mother's half hearted dinner, fell to the floor. Caroline's legs gave way and she sank back to her homework.

'Oh, don't worry,' said her mother wearily. She watched the cat explore the cheese with its tongue but made no effort to rescue it. 'Go and have a shower and then have some wine and tell me about the course.'

Her father left the room. Caroline heard the tinkle of the shower coming down the drainpipe. He had not even looked at her. She was so relieved she learned the verbs she had been told to learn and then went outside to feed the hedgehogs.

While she was spooning cat food into a hedgehog bowl she was once more aware that she was not alone. The ugly feelings of the night time engulfed her. Instinctively turning she saw Edward. He was all sunshine and smiles. He had a Sainsbury carrier bag in his hand.

'You'd better have this. It's the tin.'

'Oh, right.' She took it. Caroline found all vocabulary had gone. Her father, appearing like a missile and then retreating, had unnerved her. The night terrors had exhausted her.

'See you then.' Edward gone, she found she hated the world. She kicked the cat food tin into the heart of the flowering honeysuckle. Let it rot and spoil the scent. It was a symbol of how she now saw the world.

It was two o'clock in the morning the following Thursday. The telephone rang in the hall in the lonely moonlight. It rang to itself for a minute, as though entertaining the softly lit hall. It seemed no longer to be part of the family at this early hour. Then it penetrated everyone's dreams. Then the irregular thumping of her father's descent. Dry throated greetings from her father. A long silence. A surprisingly cheerful and wide awake goodbye ended the conversation. The ring of conclusion as the receiver was replaced finalized the moonlit interlude. Caroline heard stairs mounted two at a time.

'She's gone, Brenda. She's died. Quarter to two this morning. A massive stroke. Then heart failure.' Stark slices of facts handed to the household in general. Then the dam of her father's frustration seemed to burst. Words swirled in the moonlight.

'I couldn't have taken much more. Every night I felt I had to go and see her. All my weekends taken with work on this new project I'm doing. I was becoming stressed out with it all, at my wits' end . . . '

'It wasn't just you that was affected, Jack. What about me?' Caroline heard her mother's voice muffled with pillow and quilt. 'We'd no social life. If you didn't go and see her I did. We've not been to the theatre or the cinema since she was taken there . . . '

Caroline heard her father interrupt her. Obviously not listening to a word she said.

'I tried to ring Taylor the solicitor on Monday. I was the executor in her Will. Most of the money was left to me and all the property and the cottage. I wanted to ask him if she had altered much in that new Will she had made on Sunday morning. But he's gone off to his cottage in France.'

Caroline made a noise that she hoped conveyed her disgust. Where was the grief? Someone was dead. His vulture mind was seeing money. She made the noise again. Could see her father's pear-shaped outline by the moonlit landing window. He was an unlovely sight in skewed and wrinkled Marks and Spencers pyjamas staring out into the night. Seeing pound signs in the moonlight, she thought. He began to talk again.

'Every Sunday she would put on a hat and go to church. I wonder if she's facing her Maker now. I wonder if she's found out the truth about life and death.'

Caroline sat up, suddenly disturbed. Recalling Clara's great fear of heavenly punishment, Caroline felt an odd sensation in the pit of her stomach. Hatred for her father darkened the moonlight. She heard her mother reply with a clever quotation in French which Caroline did not understand except she heard the French word for death. Hatred for her mother eclipsed the moonlight. She saw red. She heard her father laugh at her mother's wit, heard the bed groan as he rolled back on. Then came the snores, surprisingly quickly. Had they any sensitivity?

Caroline was rigid with anger. In the end she got out of bed and slammed her bedroom door. The snoring was punctured for a while but slowly returned to full volume. Caroline rummaged in her desk and found a fluffy reel of Sellotape. Using her teeth she tore off long strands of tape and sellotaped her door to kill the grunts. She cried a little and was angry. She did not recognize grief as it visited her life for the first time.

Sleep was impossible now. And she feared the return of the invisible ones, the family tribe who watched in the dark of last Sunday. She took a chair to the window, drew back the curtains and opened the window to the night. She felt better at once and took in long breaths of the cool night air. She relaxed on the chair, leaned back, slumped. Suddenly she turned and saw the carrier bag containing Clara's tin. It had been left on the floor. Caroline had wanted nothing more to do with Clara's tortured life. But now, in the silence of the clean moonlight she found she did. She fetched the bag and opened the grimed tin. With almost tender movements she spread out the relics of Clara's grim early life on the windowsill. She let the moonlight wash over it.

The shoebox card with the trial of Edward pasted on to it, the soiled golden silk flowers from an Easter egg Clara's uncle had bought her, the blue glass beads bought on a trip to Bakewell market, the handsome photograph of the strong innocent man Clara had unwittingly sent to his death . . . All there. All of Clara's lifetime burden that was now Caroline's. Everything there in the eternal light of the moon. And what was it all for? What was it all about? Caroline found she did not know, she just did not know or understand.

Hands cupped on her chin, leaning on the windowsill with the relics of life close by, Caroline watched the morning sky. Watched it flush red but whether for anger or shame Caroline could not tell. Suddenly she saw the light of the moon had gone. The moon was now a white toy ball tossed carelessly in the blue of the west. And still, after hours and hours, she found she did not understand life and death. What was it for? Golden light illuminated the treetops in her garden.

Suddenly her tired and bewildered eyes noticed the moon had vanished. Lost to the sky and her. Vanished for ever it seemed. That universal loss suddenly released the tears and she sobbed quietly for half an hour or more, then crept into bed and fell fast asleep.

On Sunday evening Caroline discovered herself breaking all the rules. She was ringing long and hard on Edward's doorbell. She was brazen and bold, suddenly overflowing with confidence. Edward's father answered, smiling, took her into the kitchen where he was cooking Italian food with deft organization. Italian bread smells, fresh coffee in her hands. Edward appeared next, smiling and relaxed. Caroline heard herself speak and was amazed at her boldness. Some distant watcher in her brain softly wondered if this would blow apart any relationship with Edward of any kind.

'Edward, I need a bunch of wild flowers from Derbyshire. For Aunt Clara.'

Civilized negotiations about cars and meals and Edward's father watching them go as he reached and sipped a glass of wine from the kitchen. Then a long and silent journey in soft spring rain with Caroline convinced she had gone too far this time. Yet despite this Caroline felt oddly uncaring.

Edward took her to the little wood they had passed when they had wheeled Clara up the long hill to Moonfields. Caroline had not known that was where she wanted to get the flowers from until Edward stopped by it.

'Thanks, Edward.' He stayed in the driving seat as she climbed out into wind and rain. She climbed into the little wood. Putting her foot down she became stuck and ripped her jeans on barbed wire. Caroline swore viciously but so intent was she on Clara's flowers she did not look back to note Edward's reaction.

She picked the rain-wet flowers. Flowers no longer to be found in the fields with their weedkillers, pesticides, and nitrogen dressings. Clovers, daisies, orchids, sorrel, bedstraws, wild parsleys . . . Surely this was the kind of bunch Clara would have picked for school. Or on the night that swine of the other man had attempted to abuse her. Anger at that memory made her rest. She looked up and saw an old farmer patiently watching her from the fence.

'That's private land you'm on, lady. Miss Walton'd skin thee alive if she were to hear of it. Go on. Gerrout of it.'

'I am Miss Walton's great-niece. The flowers are for her.'

The farmer made a noise and turned and left. Caroline stood in the rain and arranged her flowers. She thought she had never seen such a beautiful bunch. Caroline wondered vaguely about how Clara's childhood had been such a mix of savagery and beauty. Despite the steady rain she found she was reluctant to leave the wood. There was a big stone trough with a rough stone cross carved on it. Of course. Clara's farm was called Monksbarn. Then, much later, Uncle Edward must have bought this wood with its clean spring for there was an earthenware pipe leading the water from the trough into the next field. The world groaned with the history of itself. So much there pressing in. She could feel it and hurriedly made for the car.

'Thanks, Edward.'

'That's OK.'

She saw his face was closed. She wondered again if she had smashed the special relationship she had with Edward. He started the engine with a soft rattle of the keys. She found herself hoping all would be well with her and Edward. But found the old panic of doing the right thing had gone. She found she now saw the world differently. Things could not be resolved in a minute. Sometimes, like Clara, things took a lifetime to evolve. She settled back into the comfortable front seat and smiled once at Edward when he gave her a quick glance at a crossroads.

Thirteen

'There is absolutely no need for you to come to the funeral, Caroline. It's not as if you were close to her. Your mother and myself will be representative enough.'

The atmosphere in the house was crackling with power struggles like high voltage cables before a storm. Caroline became speechless for a moment at her father's pomposity.

'But I want to go.'

'Just to get a day off school, I suppose.' His voice sounded jerky like corks popping off bottles full of intense pressure. Old suspicions hummed and buzzed in the air. Frayed and ancient hatreds seemed to be energizing her father that morning. Caroline directed death rays at her parents. She had never attended a family funeral before or any other. Clara's seemed a good one to begin with. She sighed loudly to register contempt for her parents.

Contempt had flowered early that morning. She had seen her mother sitting in front of her dressing table mirror amidst a mountain of squalid make-up bottles, some bottles as old as Caroline. Caroline had watched her do her face. Painting by numbers, she had thought. Shovelling make-up on her face, laying it on with a trowel. Now she eyeballed her father, tightly bound in a suit of dark cloth from the 1980s. An old fossil but still breathing heavily and laboriously.

'If you are going you're *not* going like that, Caroline.'

'What's wrong with what I'm wearing?' Caroline felt genuinely injured. She had selected a black top and dark trousers with some care. You were supposed to wear black for funerals, weren't you?

'If you can't see what's wrong with that get-up there's no point in talking about it.'

'Well, that's solved that then. I'll wear this.'

Caroline stalked from the room blown along by her mother's perfumed sigh of despair. She went out of the back door and was pleased to see the wild flowers she had put in a bucket of water were still as fresh as when she had picked them from Clara's wood. She returned to the kitchen and took the *Sunday Times* Business section from the debris in the kitchen. This bit of the paper was the only section her mother left untouched. She wrapped her flowers in its pages. She noticed her mother and father staring in amazement. She took the flowers and sat in the back of the car, unspeaking, splendidly sulky.

Well Cottage was packed with Waltons. Caroline watched her father give out sherry to them all as if he owned the cottage. Which he probably does now, thought Caroline, pulling a face at the taste of the sherry. It tasted absolutely foul, she thought. She looked around at the family, many of whom she had never seen before. Saw the dagger stare of old great-great-grandmother Walton passed on to several faces but did not recognize she had it too. Or Clara had. She saw Uncle Edward's handsome looks on a few faces in different generations. Caroline saw the pale blue eyes, hard in some faces, soft in others. Suddenly the whole crowd disgusted her. Panic came next. She could feel the family power just as she had felt it in the darkness of her bedroom that horrible night. She turned her back. She would like to destroy them all. She felt the panic grow.

'I need a bathroom.'

The disgust in her loud announcement turned faces in her direction. Sherry glasses approaching mouths were lowered. The prefuneral subdued talk faltered a little. They all watched Caroline launch herself from the room like a missile intent on destruction.

She landed in Edward's room, the room where Clara had tortured herself with the memory of the man she had loved and killed. The room had been stripped. 'Plundered,' muttered Caroline out loud. Cardboard boxes stood around. Anger exploded at her father. She knew he had been out to the cottage once or twice. The big picture of Uncle Edward and Clara had been turned round. A soot-stained cord and torn brown paper met her gaze. Caroline made straight for this target of her father's fear and turned it back again. And there was Clara again, sweet faced, adoring Edward, untouched by the poison that was to come.

Footsteps creaked on the stairs and Caroline heard the murmur of voices. One of the voices belonged to Fossil in his naff suit. Caroline slid from the room, quiet as the ghosts that lived in there. She fastened the bathroom door with a click. Then she bent down to listen and watch through a very big eighteenth century keyhole. Fossil was talking loudly and with authority.

'God knows why the old woman kept this room. Like a bloody shrine . . . '

'He left the cottage to Clara, you know.' A voice she did not know. 'But the housekeeper Rose was given the use of it for as long as she needed it. She lived here till the 1960s when she died. Then Clara retired here from Manchester. It was Rose who set up the room. Bed all made ready for him. Boots polished by the side of the bed. Razors ready for him to shave. The idea gives you the creeps. And Clara when she came to live here kept the room just as Rose did. It was as though she wanted him to be alive with her. Like something out of *Great Expectations*. I mean to say, he was a murderer and . . . well . . . never mind all that.'

Fossil's voice reached Caroline's ears, this time shaking with anger not with fear of threatening ghostly relics.

'I left a gold watch chain on the bedside table. His I suppose. Meant to take it with me and forgot on Friday night. Now it's gone. I bet one of them from downstairs has been up here and nicked it. People are like vultures at a funeral or a death.'

'Listen who's talking,' muttered Caroline. Then the other voice again.

'That photograph ought to be burned, Jack. Get rid of him altogether . . . '

'Over my dead body,' whispered Caroline. Then Fossil's voice again.

'I've thought of that, Harold. Trouble is that would fetch a bit in an antique shop. Still, perhaps you're right. Considering what he did and what he did to the family name . . . We don't want all that dragged out again. Mind you, these days nobody would bat an eyelid at what he did. All he would have got was ten years in prison for the murder. But I'll burn it.'

Caroline was steaming with rage behind the door. She had the sensation she would boil over soon. More voices could be heard on the stairs. There was now a chorus of voices.

'Is that girl of yours still spending a penny?'

('YES,' screamed Caroline through the keyhole, her voice as strident and penetrating as a whistling kettle boiling over.)

'Did the old woman make a Will, Jack?'

' . . . must have been worth a bit . . . '

' . . . all that land he left her . . . '

'Two woods, this cottage, no end of fields he'd bought. And Lily was saying Clara would never touch a penny of the money he left her. Invested it all. There must be nearly half a million, Fred was saying, because he saw her bankbook that day . . . '

Caroline heard Fossil's voice quell the chorus of excited speculation.

'Well, it was no secret she said she would leave it all to me. But the odd thing is Taylor has been on holiday. She made a new Will the Sunday before she died. Anyway the strange thing is Taylor rang this morning and said he wants to see me and Caroline sometime this week. God knows why. Or what it's got to do with Caroline, unless the old woman has left Caroline a few hundred or something. I did not ask the other partners in the firm. I'll wait for Taylor. The fewer people who know our business the better. I don't want any more rattling of our skeletons in our cupboard.'

More murmurs about money. More talk of Wills. Caroline left the keyhole and used the lavatory as loudly as she could. She could not believe all this talk of money on the day of Clara's funeral. All that Clara had suffered and here were these carrion crows hovering.

She yanked with fury at the lavatory chain, a long chain with a pot ball on the end like a giantess's earring. She pulled so hard that the cistern up above shifted on its bracket pulling at the old lead pipe. The pipe began to drip on the floor. Then the drip became a trickle. A graceful curving silver spout developed next. A pool appeared on the floor. Caroline flung open the door. Heard a fragment of speculation about Clara's wealth. The lid of her temper blew clean off.

'Daddy,' (with great sarcasm), 'the toilet's leaking. You'll have to spend some of Clara's pennies on it. You know, all the vast wealth everyone says she has instead of grieving for her. Excuse me.' She pushed her way through the small crowd on the landing queuing for the lavatory and the discussion of the lottery of Clara's Will.

'Excuse me. Excuse me. I've just come for the funeral.' She descended the stairs and the old oak treads murmured and groaned in sympathy. At the foot of the staircase she found herself crying. Through her tears she saw two huge ravens in black. Then blinked the blur of tears away and saw they were two men. They both gave graveyard smiles. She realized they were undertakers. She heard Fossil thumping hastily down the stairs.

'Caroline. Come here this instant. I will not have—' He caught sight of the undertakers who promptly made a speech.

'Good morning, everyone. We've been looking after Onty for the last few days. Now she's safe in her coffin and we're all ready to take her and you up to the church.'

Caroline smothered the urge to suck her thumb. She felt five years old amidst the throng of relatives. Two more black ravens appeared and to Caroline's great horror she saw on the gravel path a coffin on a polished trolley. She watched dumbly, thumb twitching towards her mouth as two distant farming relatives moved forwards. Her father thrust her to one side with 'Mind, Caroline' and made his way to the coffin also. She fixed him with wasp-sting eyes. He cleared his throat.

'Clara asked for the old way of doing things. Just like they did in the Derbyshire of her childhood. Probably the last one of this type of funeral we'll ever see.'

Two undertakers knelt down and two Walton cousins knelt behind. The coffin was expertly lowered on their shoulders. Then they stood upright with the coffin held high.

'Are we all ready, ladies and gentlemen? Everybody here?'

'There's probably a few still in there drinking that awful vinegar,' said Caroline. The words tumbled out for she was now wild with grief and her first confrontation with the rituals of death.

'My, young lady, but you've a tongue just like Clara. You should be with your dad. Go on.' Clara felt herself being pushed and very firmly too. When she was deposited by her father's side she was not sure how she had got there. She turned to laser the pusher seeing a fat image of her own genes with a hat sculpted of black wire netting. Huge glasses, miracles of optical engineering, flashed light in her direction but the eyes behind were not unkind.

Gross embarrassment followed. The coffin was carried down the street to the main road. Behind it her mother and father. Then Caroline and Aunty Nellie with the glasses and wire netting. Caroline had met her match. The woman steered Caroline by a subtle arrangement of nudges, glares, and mutterings about Walton temper as seen in Clara, Caroline, and old Grandmother Walton. Along the main road they went. Tourist traffic stopped. After a lifetime, into the churchyard. She heard the whirr of a tourist's video. Caroline searched the staring tourists with radar eyes but could not locate it. Caroline felt her face pulsate with heat and shame and she became aware of the slow tolling of the great tenor bell of the town church. It produced shivers down her back despite a two kilowatt face.

Onwards and upwards with the snailpace speed of funerals and eternity. And the great bell that was disturbing her stomach. Sunshine scorched her back now, she should have put on Factor Thirty. She'd have a rash. Then a waft of cool mildew and they were in the medieval cave of the church, the bell faint but even more disturbing, and combining with rumbling organ music, turned her guts to watery shudders. Down the long aisle went the procession, Nellie still very much in charge. Caroline twitched her shoulders.

'Put them flowers on the coffin before you take your pew,' hissed Nellie. 'I expect that's what you've brought them for.'

Escape from Nellie brought cold courage. It was cool in the big church. Seeing her mother all alone in a big pew at the very front she knew that was where she must go. Now to deliver the wild flowers. She walked alone, across the ancient tiles and laid the flowers on the coffin. Caroline turned to go and saw one of the raven men flutter and remove the flowers.

'Strictly no flowers. Miss Walton's wishes. I'll donate these to the church.' He removed the Business News and began to fold fussily with the flowers at his feet. Caroline flew at him like a hornet aware of her heart and the tenor bell overhead beating in her brain.

'Those flowers stay on her coffin. It was a bunch like that she picked before . . . before . . . she died.' She had nearly said 'before the man got her when she was twelve'.

Fossil was by her side, she could smell his aftershave and hear his heavy breathing. 'Don't start, Caroline.'

'I'm not starting. I'm finishing things off. I want those flowers on the coffin.'

Her father conceded defeat. He nodded at the undertaker. Caroline moved to the coffin with the flowers and gingerly put them on top. Caroline found her lips moving, whispering to Clara.

'Goodnight . . . Goodnight. Don't worry. If there's Anything up there They'll understand.'

Somehow she found her way back to the pew. Fifteenth-century tiles looked blurred as she walked, magnified by tears. She was aware of more coming. When she looked up to shake them away she saw one of the ravens arranging her flowers. A moonpenny daisy had strayed and was being manipulated back. Hot stares from Caroline dried the tears. Tears did not return until a miserable Victorian hymn 'The Day Thou Gavest, Lord, has Ended . . . ' Clara's day had never properly begun. Caroline struggled with tears during a boring talk about Clara and libraries.

And when she thought it was all over, it wasn't. Out in the sunlight after the church service she was hustled by Nellie into a huge car with her silent mother and father. The most comfortable car she had ever travelled in followed a car containing Clara's coffin all the way to Sheffield. Everyone clambered out of cars and into a small church and another service. Caroline was seriously bored now and a savage headache was growing. She would have journeyed along with Clara into the great unknown if there had been a Mars bar at the end. She developed uncontrollable fidgets which produced stares from Fossil, and 'I told you not to bother coming,' from her mother.

Then a profound shock. The coffin had been on a tiny stage with a spotlight. Suddenly the coffin began to slide inwards with the wild flowers on top. A pair of curtains like those on a Punch and Judy stage began to close as the coffin gathered speed. Then closed. Caroline knew very well where the coffin was going. Straight into the gas flames of the cremating oven. She sat down and covered her face with her hands. On the way back she bit the nails of her right hand down to the quick—a habit she had thought conquered when she was eleven.

Clara's old-fashioned sitting room was packed with food when they returned to Well Cottage. Waitresses with professionally mournful smiles were ready to serve food. The adults were making a noise much louder than a school dinner room. Caroline was squinting with a pounding headache, sick with grief and hunger. Despite the growing noise of chatter she saw the number of relatives had declined. Two children, five and seven perhaps, not noticed before, raced round the cottage. Their father was struggling to control them and failing. Caroline felt a little more herself as the children, Peter and Wendy, played hide and seek around Fossil, their father yanking, nagging, apologizing. A spark of hunger grew into an all-consuming appetite.

The waitresses were eager to pile her plate with a well constructed mountain of food. The base of the mountain a circular foothill of something the women called vol-aux-vents, tiny volcanoes of puffed pastry with creamed prawns in their craters. Two chicken legs made a north face of the mountain, which was snow-capped with white bread sandwiches. Caroline made a vow to return in haste for the Arctic Roll already quarried by Peter and Wendy, the evidence showing round their mouths. Caroline eyed the white wine while trying to hypnotize the tiny boulders of radishes not to avalanche down the mountain.

'You can have some wine, dear, as long as father says so.'

'Yes, he says so.' Caroline gave her three star smile usually reserved for when she saw Edward. Then carefully steering away from Fossil she navigated the shoals of relatives and headed for the hall. She liked the staircase. She would sit on the warm oak stairs.

Caroline settled down and sipped the wine with satisfaction. But Peter and Wendy kept whizzing by like a manic version of *Peter Pan*. The second time round she fixed them with a Captain Hook scowl and they flitted back to the Arctic Roll followed by their father pursuing his darlings. Caroline sniffed and attacked the mountain. After a few minutes she climbed the stairs to the top. Spotting Wendy fluttering and searching for a lavatory Caroline swore and took her food and wine into Edward's room.

She sat on the very hard bed and gnawed ferociously on a chicken leg. Her mind gnawed at Clara's life. Clara, she thought, had been a female Peter Pan. Everything had stopped at twelve. She had lived in a darkened land where nothing would ever flourish. A Never Never Land indeed.

Eating a slice of succulent chicken pie she decided she hated this room. In fact she loathed it. It smelled of dust and misery. A mean triangle of sunshine shone on the brown painted windowsill. She knew that was all the room would ever get. Beyond was the view of the graveyard and the frowning east end of the church. The room was a time capsule of everything wrong with Clara's early twentieth century childhood. Caroline abruptly stood up. A pickled onion fell. Oh, leave it, she thought. Fossil could sweep it later. She went out.

She could hear Wendy in the bathroom. She made a crocodile noise at the door. Then she saw a small door in the wall. A door to the attic. She opened it. Caroline saw tiny stairs twisting like Victorian barley sugar sticks. She stooped through the door and closed it. She noticed a heavy eighteenth century bolt and locked it and went up to the attic with the remains of her mountain and wine. Then she almost dropped the lot when she reached the attic.

The attic was a long low room as big as the cottage area. Sunshine everywhere cascading in through a large circular window. A view of sandstone slabbed rooftops and chimneys and then distant woodlands. Moving closer to the window Caroline saw the room looked down on to the Butter Market. Caroline was totally entranced by it and sat down in a very comfortable white armchair, vintage 1970 Habitat. Books were everywhere, shelves of them, tottering piles of them. An expensive tape recorder was surrounded by a chaos of audio books used by Clara when her eyesight failed. Caroline looked with professional admiration at the disorder. Here Clara had let herself go. Caroline sipped her wine. And was glad. Clara had had something out of life.

Caroline slowly became aware of the many children's books, C.S. Lewis, Nesbit, several editions of *Wind in the Willows*. Poor Clara. Perhaps the child under twelve in her was the only happy bit of her savaged life. Caroline eyed the huge double radiator and realized Clara must have spent hours up here. Then she suddenly spotted a silver frame with a postcard-size picture of Uncle Edward in it. She thought that up here Clara had got things in perspective whereas downstairs in that horrid room . . . she shuddered.

There was a little side table with a copy of *Great Expectations* on it and underneath a tiny waste-paper basket stuffed with Mars bar wrappers. Lighter coloured ones revealing Clara's taste for the ice cream variety. Everything was coated with dust. Caroline's spirits soared. So Clara had found some pleasure in life, some escape. Caroline found the grief that had whined like toothache in her mind was gone. This room with its dust, its armchair, its books was . . . she struggled for words . . . beautiful. She leaned back, glad and happy and relieved. She had frankly been terrified by the prospect of Clara's life. But Clara had found an oasis. She suddenly felt very, very hungry again.

Opening the attic staircase door she saw the startled eyes of Peter and Wendy arrested in mid flight.

'What's in there?'

'Oh, dragons, monsters, a witch . . . ' Caroline recalled Clara's shelf of C.S. Lewis first editions. 'And a lion.' She locked the door, turning a key that was in it and putting it in her pocket. Peter and Wendy fled to their father and captured at last were bustled out into the family car.

Downstairs Caroline saw Fossil flushed with wine explaining his job as executor of Clara's Will.

'Dad, am I allowed a glass of wine?'

'Yes, of course. But only one.' He was relieved there had been no scenes in the last hour.

'Thanks, Dad.'

Caroline moved to a waitress who had heard the request and got her wine. She built a second mountain of desserts and topped it with ice cream. Smiling sweetly she left the room to celebrate the return of happiness in Clara's den.

Fourteen

Caroline eyeballed the solicitor, staring at him with evil intensity. She fixed him with a dagger stare, a vintage genetic brew passed to her by Clara's Grandmother Walton. Caroline silently accused the man of being in league with her father. Today she had wanted to be at school because it was netball day. Caroline had not listened to her father's mutterings about the need to see the solicitor. She thought it was something to do with the funeral. She wished she'd never gone. No. Cancel that. She was glad she'd found Clara's gloryhole. Caroline continued her visual bombardment of Mr Taylor, Clara's solicitor. The solicitor who was to deliver Clara's treasure to her father. She squeezed her plastic coffee cup, angry with the world. A shadow of grief for Clara dimmed her mind. There was a crack like a chicken bone snapping as the plastic beaker wilted beneath Caroline's angry squeeze. A thin stream of coffee splashed on her white school blouse and rebounded on to the carpet. Caroline blushed and the tide of red swept away her daggers look.

She heard her father sigh with irritation. Caroline rekindled her anger and looked at her father as if he were a bad smell. All he thinks of is money. He's like an old tatty money bag himself. Soiled and sagging, ready to be chucked away. The thought made her smile. Her father thought this was a smirk. Anger ploughed furrows in his face. He turned away. Well, he thought, he was here for bigger things. Now was the time to sort out Clara's money. Make life a lot easier. Perhaps retire early and live in the cottage. There might be enough to buy an old farmhouse in Provence, instead of the tiny cottage the family had in Normandy. Then his furrowed face stretched in amazement.

'I give to my great-niece CAROLINE FAY WALTON of 63a Limewood Avenue, Eastcaster, my thanks and gratitude for ending for me a lifetime of suffering with her comfort and love. I give to her free of inheritance tax and absolutely my property known as Well Cottage, Church Lane, Lambton, including the furnishings and the contents thereof . . .'

Caroline was not listening. Her father was not a fossil. He was a sack of worn out ideals and ideas. He was a rubbish sack. He was . . . but her cascade of metaphorical hate suddenly dried up. The colour had drained from his face. He was sitting up very straight. Caroline was used to his avoidance tactics when she stared at him and made him uncomfortable. Going into the downstairs lavatory and slamming the door. Holding *The Times* very high in front of his face. Cleaning the oven. But today his reaction was very gratifying. Caroline missed more vital words.

'And I also leave to the said CAROLINE FAY WALTON my fields in the Parish of One Ash, in the County of Derbyshire, west of the farm known as Moonfields Farm, the fields known as Daisy Field, Mouse Park, Elbow, and Butterfield . . .'

To Caroline's alarm her father turned to her and looked. She thought he was going to vomit. Consternation and alarm blew out the satisfaction she had felt earlier. And she missed the fact Clara had left her two barns, a stable, a sheep pen and a cow shed. At that point awareness dawned that the green tinted white her father had turned was not of her doing. He was on his feet now, spluttering, hissing. Broken words spattering out at Mr Taylor. That gentleman was blinking fast behind his glasses. Caroline was diverted and fascinated by the creases on her father's jacket.

'You're telling me that the old fool altered her Will at the last minute and left the whole bloody lot to Caroline?'

Still the meaning was lost to her. As a student of her father's rages she noted how the word 'Caroline' stuck in his throat. How her name produced in him a tiny asthma attack. It was far more interesting than Mr Taylor's tiny droning voice.

'So, Caroline's got everything? Cottage, fields, money, shares, the lot? The old fool must have been out of her mind. I shall have a long talk with my daughter here. She hardly knew the old woman except to see her at the end. As I said, I'll have a long talk with madam here and we'll see about contesting the Will and going back to the original one that left the bulk to me.'

Caroline had heard. She had gone cold. Cold as Edward's room. Cold as a tombstone. But the mention of 'madam' brought a hot eruption of steamy hatred for her father again. Then the feeling that Clara had left her a huge burden, not just money but knowledge. She knew how Eve felt in Eden when the snake introduced knowledge.

'And why in Hell's name has she left my next door neighbour's son five thousand pounds? That proves the old idiot was out of her mind.'

At the mention of Edward's name Caroline was fully alert, wanting all the details now.

'I think not, Jack.' Mr Taylor was both steely and authoritative. Generations of his family had sat in this same office and made the wills of generations of Waltons. Only the carpets and the rows of plastic dummy books had changed. He cleared his throat.

'No, Jack. When she called me in that morning, not long before she died, I disagree, she was perfectly sane. In fact I've never seen her more relaxed despite the end being near. The matron and a doctor witnessed the new Will. You would be wasting your time and money if you contest this Will. And don't forget that you are the executor and trustee. You will look after things until Caroline is twenty-one.'

In reply to this her father gave a strangled sob and rushed out on to the landing. There he stood with his hands in his pockets, slumped, staring out of the window. Mr Taylor showed surprising cool.

'Caroline. May I suggest you have a look round the market. It's market day here in the town. Say, about half an hour. Your father and I have documents to sign. Then, if you come back you can have more coffee and sign some papers for me.'

Her father kept his back to her. Out in sunshine she curiously felt Clara had pushed her into a family trap. She walked towards the butter market and ignored the stalls thronged with tourists. Instead she stood at the bottom of a flight of steps leading to Church Lane and the cottage that was now hers. She felt no sense of pleasure.

Then her eye caught the round window of Clara's den. True, Clara had handed over a secret as heavy as lead, poisonous as nuclear waste. A secret that would need a sarcophagus of control as heavy as the concrete poured over the horrors of Chernobyl. Yet Clara had rewarded her. The sun sparkled on the round window. Caroline suddenly realized how nice it must be up there on a sunny morning. And it was hers.

She bought a huge stick of candyfloss. Surrounded by spun sugar and sunlight Caroline sat on the butter market steps and looked up at Clara's window on life.

To Caroline's amazement it was her mother who came to her rescue, placed a peace-keeping force between Caroline's father and his daughter.

After all, she pointed out, the money was still in the family. They could still use Well Cottage as a holiday cottage until Caroline reached the old age of twenty-one. The money in trust would pay for any further education Caroline would want. 'And I don't need to tell you, Jack, that it costs thousands these days to send someone to university. We shan't have that problem. Clara's money will pay for all that.' Caroline had heard her mother pause. Probably to let the facts sink into her father's fossilized brain. Then 'She could go to Oxford or Cambridge with all the money she has. And unlike other poor students the cash would actually buy her a flat or house while she was a student. No accommodation problems or money to find.'

Caroline, intent, eager at the keyhole, heard her father snort. She heard his mirthless laugh.

'Huh. Huh. Can you see Caroline at a university? I can't. She'll be lucky if she gets a pass in anything. Oral English perhaps, with that mouth and lip of hers.'

Caroline exuded killer X-rays through the door. That was it. Oxford here I come, she thought. No. The university that Edward went to. She'd go there. And if it was Oxford, she'd be there. And suddenly a still, small, cold thought bubbled up. Clara had wanted to make something of her life, go to Cambridge or something. But chance had been throttled when Edward had hanged. Now, she, Caroline, had the freedom and money to go where she wanted. Somehow it would be disloyal to Clara not to do her best, make something of life.

The family did use Clara's cottage as a holiday cottage. Caroline made very sure that all her mother's junk piled up in Edward's room. Dirty washing, cardboard boxes, carrier bags—Caroline gleefully tidied up her cottage and piled up her mother's detritus. It laid ghosts like water on dust. She let her father sell the menacing cut-throat razors and other Edwardian artifacts. But she hid the picture from her father's grasp.

'Well, I don't know where that picture's gone. The same

way as the gold watch. I only wanted to sell it and put the money in your Trust.' And Caroline had smiled, wise to the world and a century of misery.

She had demanded the attic for herself. She loved it, cherished the dust and books. Clara had ignored the dust of the world in the same way as Caroline. Except for a futon she demanded to sleep on, the attic was kept just as it was. She made sure the waste basket was always well stuffed with Mars wrappers. It was a room that seemed to attract the sunlight just as Edward's room below stealthily absorbed any shadows of the day that were available.

Later still when she was doing her A levels at college she went to her cottage at weekends on her own. Edward would come down from his medical school as often as he could. Caroline placed a tatty sleeping bag in Uncle Edward's room. Not that Edward ever slept in it . . . But she liked to tell her father that it was 'Edward's room' so she could see the family skeleton rattle in his brain and make him go white. Caroline was well into her twenties before she abandoned the habit of a lifetime of teasing her father's fossilized hang-ups inherited from a tight-minded century.

Yet Caroline never lost the hatred for Edward's room. It symbolized for her all that was wrong with the earlier part of the old century when Clara had been a lost child on those high hills of the western White Peak of Derbyshire. She considered it a page of family history to be torn out and thrown away—but for totally different reasons to her father. Like the diaries. She'd found Clara's diaries in a chest in her attic. They proved how Clara's life had been as viciously strangled as Edward's neck by the rope.

WEDNESDAY 14 MARCH 1951

Grey & dull. Rain all day. Library from 8 until 6-30. Tea with Edna at Lewis's.

Home at 8. Bath. Reading Wordsworth's 'Prelude' again.

THURSDAY 15 MARCH 1951
Day off. Caught 8-53 train at Central. Arrived Monsal Dale 9-45. Walked in strong sun to Chelmorton. Ate sandwiches there. Larks singing, plovers calling. A few celandines. Then walked to High Needham. Then down past Moonfields. Caught train from Parsley Hay to Buxton. Back in London Road station Manchester at 6. Glorious sunset over Axe Edge.

Clara had passed the farm where she had accidentally killed two men. Not a breath of it in the diary. How could she, how could she keep the hell fires burning in her brain from scorching the page? One by one Caroline destroyed the tight little leather bound diaries with emotions held in predictable rein, as clockwork as the moon's phases that littered the pages of the diaries. One by one she took the strangled years from 1941 to 1990 when they stopped. The earlier ones had been lost in a Nazi bombing raid on Manchester. She learned that from sly questions to her father.

All she wanted was the true part of Clara's life. The picture of her smiling up at Edward and the marvellous books she had collected. Books where emotions and feelings erupted like hot lava boiling from the page. That was the real Clara, as real as she could get. Rip and burn those lost years through the century.

In the future Caroline, Edward, and their children used the cottage as a holiday cottage. Caroline always made sure tents, wet clothes, walking boots, and dirty washing accumulated in Edward's room. Even in her forties she saw it as a detestable tomb of a room.

Later still Edward became a Consultant in Geriatric Care at a big hospital in the Midlands. They had the money to buy the cottages on either side and restore the property to its original title of Well House. Browsing in the library Caroline discovered that a daughter of an apothecary had lived there and been accused of witchcraft. The house had been turned into three cottages at the so-called witch's death. Clara's Grandmother Walton had bought one of the cottages. Clara had hinted that Grandmother Walton was a fearsome woman. It gave Caroline pleasure to see herself as a continuing line of difficult women living in the property.

During the conversion back into the eighteenth century house Caroline at last turned Edward's room into another bathroom. She felt as if a burden was lifted from her. Clara's ball and chain were snapped. But she never used the bathroom herself.

The attic stayed as it was except they all added their books to it. It was a family rule that you went up there alone and you were not to be disturbed in your thoughts. It was a room to help you live with yourself, Caroline told her children.

As for the picture of Edward and Clara, she had it properly restored as soon as she was twenty-one and did not have to ask her father for Clara's money. She put him and Clara in the hall. You saw them as soon as you entered the house. Caroline always put a vase of wild flowers there in May and June when the farmers used to grow the grass for hay. Buttercups, moonpenny daisies, clover, vetch, grasses. Complainers of hayfever received dagger looks if they dared to complain about the pollen laden blooms.

And she told her children the story, every bit of it. But they were told never to mention it to their grandad.

'Why?' asked Jack the youngest who was very fond of his grandfather.

'Because he learned some sad ideas and they became fossils. And you can easily damage fossils. You don't want to hurt him, Jack, do you?'

For many years she thought of asking for a pardon for Edward Walton. But reading the court case in the Record

Office at Matlock she realized the evidence against Edward still looked safe. Only Clara had known the truth and could have testified and pardoned him—but at the same time convicting herself. The truth had burned with her in the flames of the crematorium. And on some days, much against her better judgement, Caroline found herself praying that the flames in the crematorium were the only flames Clara would ever see.

Acknowledgements

I would like to thank Mary and Rebecca Green for helping me with the typescript of *Daggers*. Without their patient help the book would not exist.

Also by Roger J. Green

Cuckoos ISBN 0 19 271792 8

'You'll die for this. I'll lock you up in my den for this.'
John's threats were like a cuckoo's egg. Once laid, they stayed there and pushed everything else out of your life.

Sam Wilkinson has become the latest target of John Snow's bullying tactics. Even though there is no physical violence, John's threats and insults have the power to bring Sam's world crashing down around him. And when nobody will listen, Sam decides the time has come for him to take action. But Sam's attempt to stand up for himself has consequences that could not have been foreseen, especially by John . . .

'*Cuckoos* depicts a frighteningly realistic contemporary scenario . . . Green is as intent on getting inside the mind of the bully as the victim.'

The Times Educational Supplement

'*Cuckoos* is full of cruelly accurate comments on the ways adults fail to hear children crying for help.'

The Times

The Throttlepenny Murder ISBN 0 19 275052 6

Jessie hated old Throttlepenny, her mean-spirited boss. She spent her days dreaming of ways to hurt him, but she'd never have the nerve to turn her dreams into reality.

But Throttlepenny is murdered. It's Jessie that the police come for, and Jessie that winds up in jail. Will someone prove her innocence—before she's hanged?

' . . . a most compelling novel.'

Junior Bookshelf

' . . . a cleverly plotted thriller, misleading the reader in several directions right up to the end.'

The Times Literary Supplement

'The narrative is gripping. There is descriptive writing of a very high quality . . . '

School Librarian

Other Oxford children's novels

Vixen's Haunt Frankie Calvert
ISBN 0 19 271807 X

It is Vixen's thirteenth birthday morning when her mother turns up unexpectedly. Vixen lives quite happily and calmly with her father. Her mother constantly travels the world, and Vixen very rarely sees her. This time, however, the surprise visit is only the beginning. It starts up a chain of events which lead Vixen to the most amazing discoveries.

Vixen has always loved foxes. When she was little she used to think she really was a fox. And all through her birthday summer, Vixen is haunted by the past, hunted by possible danger. But this time she can't run away.

Dark Thread Pauline Chandler
ISBN 0 19 271761 8

Kate knows the mill well. She and her mother had an exhibition of their weaving there. Before.

But that was a different life, before the accident. And now Kate knows that she just can't cope any more.

But when she suddenly finds herself back in another world that is strange and familiar all at the same time, Kate finds that she has no choice. She has to keep going, to survive, and to protect the other people in her new family. This new way of life is exhausting and unrelenting. And in the background there is always the mill, with the machines that never stop, the work which never ends, and the dangerous power that drives it.

The Tower at Moonville Stephen Elboz

ISBN 0 19 271806 1

Nathan and Sam change places. Sam goes off into the world, to seek adventure, and Nathan finds adventure of a very different kind in the strangest of all schools, Moonville. There are no teachers, no lessons, and the boys are left to run riot. Nathan meets the old scientist who lives in the tower, and he begins to learn all about the stars, the planets, and the possibility of life beyond our universe, But then Nathan's wicked uncle finally tracks him down, and life gets very dangerous indeed.

Humanzee Susan Gates

ISBN 0 19 275038 0

'He's just an animal, isn't he? But he walks upright and he looks a bit human, that's all. So I call him humanzee, half-man, half-chimpanzee, see.'

'You can't put people in cages,' said Nemo, appalled. So he persuades his parents to buy Chingwe, the humanzee, and take him with them as they tour the country with their travelling Flea Circus. But it is not so easy to cope with an old and emotionally upset humanzee, especially when the scientists want to experiment on him, and other people object to his very existence and come after him with guns. Nemo has to think fast to save Chingwe from the dangers that are threatening him.

Facing the Dark Michael Harrison

ISBN 0 19 271801 0

Simon's father has been accused of the murder of a rival cab driver and Simon faces a life branded as the son of a murderer. Then he meets Charley, grieving for her dead father, the murder victim, and they determine to find out the real story behind the murder. Together they can face up to the danger which surrounds them, and bring back some hope for the future.

Hold My Hand and Run Margaret McAllister

ISBN 0 19 271769 3

Kazy decides to run away from home and take her sister, Beth, with her. She has no choice: the beatings are getting worse; she can't protect Beth from them, and their father won't listen. Perhaps running away will be the answer.

But from the very beginning, things go wrong. Kazy and Beth can find nowhere to stay and be safe. The people chasing them, to bring them home again, are getting nearer and nearer. Kazy needs all her quick-thinking and courage to keep going. But then she and Beth find themselves facing disaster.

Kazy is desperate to do the right thing. But once you've run away, it's impossible to go back, isn't it?

The Stones are Hatching Geraldine McCaughrean
ISBN 0 19 271797 9

Phelim was the only one, they said, the only one who could save the world from the Hatchlings of the Stoor Worm. The Stoor Worm, who had been asleep for aeons, was beginning to waken. The dreadful sounds of war had roused it, and now its Hatchlings were abroad, terrorizing the people who had forgotten all about them, forgotten all the ancient magics.

But how could Phelim, who was only a boy, after all, save the world from all these dreadful monsters? And where could he find the Maiden, the Fool, and the Horse who were supposed to help him? As Phelim leaves his home and sets out on his quest, the words ring in his ears: 'You are the one. To stop the Worm waking. To do what must be done.'

Witchy Ann Phillips
ISBN 0 19 275049 6

Thrown out of home on suspicion of being a witch, twelve-year-old Aggie has to make her own way in the harsh world of the Fens in the 1890s. But wherever she goes, the gossip follows her, until she almost comes to believe it herself. 'If I got seeing and knowing,' she asks her gran, 'am I a witch?'

Befriended by the chapel-going Willetts, Aggie hopes she can put the past behind her and make a new life for herself; but then comes news from home and Aggie is thrust back into a life of superstition and hate . . .

Vicious Circle Helena Pielichaty

ISBN 0 19 271775 8

Ten-year-old Louisa May and her mother Georgette are two of the 'have-nots', shuttling between ever-seedier bed and breakfast accommodation. To help cope with this way of life they play elaborate fantasy games, pretending to be the characters in the romantic fiction that Georgette borrows from the library in every town they move to.

When they arrive at the Cliff Top Villas Hotel in a run-down seaside resort and Georgette falls ill, it looks as if the fantasy will have to end. But Louisa May enlists the help of Joanna, another hotel resident, and together they determine to find out the truth behind Georgette's 'let's pretend' existence. Maybe this way there will be a chance for them to break out of the vicious circle and become 'haves' at last . . .

Daggers

I was responsible for my mother's murder. I know I was. People would say I murdered her? What did I do? I killed her... It's true ... that dream. And I killed her.

When Caroline reluctantly goes to see her Great-Aunt Clara in the old people's home, she is unprepared for the revelations that follow. Surely her aunt must be rambling under the influence of all the medicines she is taking for the illnesses that have landed her in the home? How could this gentle old lady who had spent all her life as a librarian possibly have killed anyone?

But her aunt's confession seems to help Caroline in her own struggles to come to terms with her feelings for her parents. Is there the key to her own animosity towards her father in the past and the family history her father is so keen to keep secret?

Robert [illegible] was born in Buxton in Derbyshire in 1964. He taught for many years in Sheffield primary schools and he lives in Sheffield with his family.